THE DARK RETURN OF TIME

The Dark Return of Time

by

R. B. Russell

Swan River Press
Dublin, Ireland
MMXXIV

The Dark Return of Time
by R. B. Russell

Published by
Swan River Press
at Æon House
Dublin, Ireland
June MMXXIV

www.swanriverpress.ie
brian@swanriverpress.ie

Cover design by Meggan Kehrli
from "The Dark Return of Time" (2014)
by Jason Zerillo

Set in Garamond by Ken Mackenzie

Paperback Edition
ISBN 978-1-78380-774-1

Swan River Press published
a limited hardback edition of
The Dark Return of Time in May 2014.

For Rosalie

Part One

I.

There was a subtle change in the light. I looked up from my newspaper, aware that someone was standing in front of our small shop window. Over the top of my spectacles I could see that a man of late middle age, well-groomed and smartly dressed, was peering in at the display of Penguin modern classics. I decided that he was out of place, but I could not immediately identify why. I guessed that he was English; there was something about the way that he frowned and rubbed his chin. He presumably believed himself to be unobserved. He was interested in the books, but he also appeared to be disapproving.

And then he was gone, leaving me feeling slightly irritated. I put down the newspaper and walked over to the door. Through the glass I could see that he was on the pavement opposite, contemplating our sign that declared "Bennett's British Bookshop". He was leaning on a cane, which had to be an affectation, and my annoyance with him increased as he checked a pocket-watch on a fob chain. I was pleased to see him walk away, idly, down the rue Berthe.

It was a quarter to six. My father's shop was empty and likely to remain that way. I loved it at such moments; it seemed to exist outside of time and space. The silence was an almost physical presence among the shelves, sifting down onto the books with the dust through the soft, late afternoon light. The clock above the counter may have been ticking to itself, but it signified nothing. I treasured those fragile moments, because they could be disturbed upon an instant by the appearance of a customer.

I turned the sign on the door to *fermé*, and in the small office behind the counter I switched off the lights. My father would not be returning from his book-buying trip until late, so there was no chance of a reprimand for closing early.

Out on the constricted pavement, between the buildings and the parked cars, everything seemed somehow under pressure, waiting, expectant. A grey layer of cloud was pressed down tight like a lid on the city, reducing my awareness of it to just those few thoroughfares I needed to negotiate to return to my apartment. As usual I had an excuse to visit the Epicerie on the rue de Trois Frères, buying milk and peaches. The dark interior of the shop always smelled strongly of fruit, of earth, and indefinable spices. In some ways it reminded me of shops I had known as a child, but the French labels and packaging had an allure and an exoticism, even when they were for the most mundane of everyday provisions.

My thoughts turned to what I would be making myself for dinner that evening, and I wondered whether I would be able to resist eating one of the peaches before I reached home. Back outside it was too bright, and the passing traffic sounded loud and harsh. Across the road, however, was another haven from the noise of the city; the narrow series of stone steps down into the Passage des Abbesses.

As I descended, I was intrigued by the sight of a woman at the foot of the fourth and final flight. She was looking around uncertainly, as though lost. Her long black coat concealed her figure, and she looked away as I reached the bottom of the steps. All that I received was a glimpse of her face, and a hint of her perfume. She reminded me of Corrina.

I was a few paces into the square formed by the dog-leg in the Passage, where it opens out and is accessible to traffic from the other direction. My thoughts were of Corrina, but I still noticed the man who had so recently been standing outside my father's bookshop. He was now lounging in a doorway, looking again at his ridiculous watch.

Once again I was annoyed by the man, but at that moment, in the far corner of the courtyard, a door burst open. It crashed against a parked car and bounced back towards a large man in a balaclava who was coming out. He caught the door as it rebounded, looked around quickly, and pulled from behind him a naked, white, skinny man. His wrists were bound together with thick grey tape and he reeled from the other's grasp. Unable to save himself, he fell to the ground.

I was transfixed. A large white van was parked with its engine running, its rear doors open. The man in the balaclava lifted the naked man off the ground and flung him inside as though he was no weight at all.

Immediately afterwards another thug, similarly dressed, came out. This one was dragging a naked, gagged and bound woman. He swung her around by her pink-dyed hair and pushed her backwards into the van, jumped in, and dragged her inside. The doors closed, and immediately the engine was loud in the narrow confines of the Passage; the van drove off towards the rue des Abbesses.

"What the hell!" I shouted, suddenly able to move. I turned to my neighbour in the doorway, but he was already walking back towards the Passage steps. "We must call the police!" I insisted.

As he ignored me I assumed he must be French after all. *"Nous appeler la police!"* I called. He continued to take no notice; he was climbing the steps, apparently unconcerned.

"Appelez la police!" I called out again, rushing after him, hoping that he might have a mobile phone. He still refused to turn around, and even the woman who had reminded me of Corrina was running away, now taking the top flight two steps together. At that time of the evening there were normally dozens of people walking up and down the Passage. Now, however, it was deserted. I looked around at the high buildings that enclosed the space, at the myriad blind windows. The whole of Paris seemed not to have just been unaware of what had happened, but had turned its back on it.

To my relief, a door opened just a few feet away and an old woman in a faded floral housecoat emerged uncertainly. When I strode towards her she drew back inside, confused and perhaps worried. However, she stopped short of closing the door on me when she realised I wanted her to call the police.

I couldn't think of the French for "kidnap" so I said, *"les hommes ont pris deux personnes!"*

Her expression changed to one of concern. She suggested that I follow her inside and make the call myself. The telephone was in the corner of a dark, cluttered and dusty living room, and she watched me closely as I dialled. She then listened, with increasing disbelief, as I tried, in my halting French, to tell the operator what had happened. When I was able to put the phone down the old woman asked me to explain again what I'd seen. It was slightly easier the second time because the words had been rehearsed, and her incredulity turned to horror as she understood me.

Back out in the square people were walking through the Passage once more, quite oblivious to what had happened. The old woman made me show her the door through which the couple had been dragged. It gaped open obscenely, and in the darkness beyond all we could see were some uncarpeted stairs.

"Je ne connais pas les couples qui vivent là," she was saying. *"Mais, ils ont toujours semblé si gentil et tranquille."*

I wasn't sure that I'd grasped the tenses she had used; what she said sounded as though she blamed the couple for what had happened. She continued talking, but I gave up trying to follow her words.

The police seemed to be taking an inordinate amount of time to arrive, and the old woman accosted a neighbour who looked suspiciously out from a doorway opposite. As I listened to her describing what had happened, I began to tremble. Soon I could do nothing to stop the shaking. I knew that it had to be shock and I pressed my back against a wall, hoping to use the great mass of the building to calm myself. I felt a fool; unsure whether I'd be able to speak again without my fear being obvious.

Another neighbour came out, and then another, and they stared at me and pointed accusingly. It was comforting to finally hear the siren of an approaching police car, although I felt an unaccountable desire to flee the scene. When the police car came in through the archway from the rue des Abbesses the siren increased in volume as it echoed off the high walls, and it still rang in my ears when it was cut.

The woman took charge of the situation, telling the first policeman that I was a tourist, which I resented. However, my annoyance enabled me to explain that I *lived* in Paris. Now that it was time to give a third description of the events my words were more assured and I was able to appear relatively composed.

However, the policeman was unimpressed. When I said that I didn't know the registration number of the van he frowned and said, *"Pourquoi n'avez-vous pas noté?"* The policeman, the woman and her neighbours all shook their heads when I admitted to not even noticing what make of vehicle it was.

When I said *"Il était blanc,"* they all looked at each other and raised their eyebrows.

The exasperated policeman asked if it had any *"distinction des caractéristiques"*. When I could only shrug he asked, *"Quelle direction il a disparu quand elle est partie du passage; gauche ou droit?"*

Again all I could do was apologise and further knowing glances were exchanged between the policeman and the locals.

"Pouvez vous décrire les assaillants?" the policeman tried. I felt even more of an idiot, unable to think of a French word for balaclava.

"Y avait-il un troisième homme?" I was asked. *"Un conducteur?"*

"A conductor?" I thought, and realised that he was asking about the driver. I couldn't have described him even if I was sure there had been a third man.

"Étaient ils ont armé?" he asked seriously, and mimicked a man firing a gun.

I shook my head, but I wasn't sure. I closed my eyes and tried to picture them, each assailant using one hand to pull the people out of the building. The first had dragged the man out by the arm, the second the woman by the hair. I told the policeman that I thought they might have been carrying guns.

During the fruitless cross-examination, his partner had entered the building and returned to report that there had been a *"combat"*, a fight in the apartment.

I noticed blood on the ground where the kidnapped man had fallen.

"L'homme nude," I said, knowing that the word wasn't quite right. *"L'homme de l'intérieur, il est tombé à la terre,*

là," I pointed. "Blood." Already it had dried and was not so obvious on the stone setts. I repeated "*Sang*", not sure if he understood. I was flustered; all the words sounded absurd in my mouth; French and English.

The first policeman dismissed the onlookers who merely retreated a few paces. The other patiently asked: "Did anyone else see what happened?"

I was irritated that I had struggled to speak in French to his colleague when this man obviously understood me.

"Yes, there was a man in the doorway over there," I said. "He would've seen everything."

"And where is he now?"

"He went back up the steps towards the Trois Frères."

"Can you describe him?"

"Late middle-age, grey hair, smart suit with a waistcoat. He was carrying a cane . . . "

The policeman was incredulous: "You can describe the witness, but not the criminals?"

"Yes," I agreed, ashamed.

"Was there anyone else?"

"A woman, coming down the steps, but she turned and hurried away." An image of Corrina came into my mind, but I fought to dismiss it. "She had long dark hair and was wearing a black coat . . . but she probably wouldn't have seen anything from up there, at that angle."

I gave my name and address, and all the time further cars arrived and more policemen appeared, demanding and receiving explanations. I was able to follow this quite well, and understood the insulting description of me as a foreigner. I was told to sit in the back of one of the cars.

The attitudes of the various policemen annoyed me and I decided that I would wait *beside* the car rather than get in it. An officer was putting up tape between the two No Parking signs on either side of the entrance to the Passage, causing people to stop in the rue des Abbesses and look in at what might be happening.

Time passed slowly. I was nervous; the idea of more questions filled me with dread and I was beginning to wish that I'd ignored what I'd seen, just as the man with the cane and fob-watch had done. I had always felt that Paris was a friendly city, but now it seemed quite hostile. Although I had thought that I was a part of it, I was being reminded that I was a foreigner.

"Your name is Flavian Bennett?" the plain-clothes policeman asked, in very good English, once I had been called over.

"Yes. I have an apartment on the rue André Antoiné."

"And you are English? What sort of name is Flavian?"

"It's Roman. They were Emperors. My father . . . "

"So, you saw everything, but can't describe the kidnappers or their vehicle?"

"No."

"You were just passing?"

"I work on rue Berthe. I was on my way home."

"Can you describe the people they took away?"

"They were both young; in their twenties or thirties. He had long dark hair and was unshaven, very skinny. She was short, perhaps a little fat, with dyed pink hair."

"They were naked?"

"Yes. They looked like they'd been beaten."

"Did they have any facial piercings?"

"I don't know. I was over there," I pointed. "It all happened very quickly."

"Show me."

I took him to where I had been standing and explained, "I could see the door and the back of the van. I had a clear view, but it was distant."

The policeman produced a photograph and I put on my spectacles.

"You weren't wearing those before?" he asked. "That's why you didn't see anything?"

I didn't answer; the glasses were only for reading, but I was happy to have an excuse. Instead of answering I stared at the photograph, which showed a young couple sitting together on the grass. They were in some sort of park or garden and were grinning at the camera.

"I'm sure that's them," I confirmed, putting my glasses away.

The man glanced around and up at all the windows in the high walls. By now there were plenty of people staring out at what was happening below.

"And the other witness was standing in this doorway here?" he asked.

"Yes."

"You say he was old. Grey hair, well dressed, with a cane?"

"Not so old; late middle-aged. He hurried away back up there . . . "

The policeman nodded.

"Thank you, Mr. Bennett. You can go now. We have your address and may wish to talk to you again. But it seems unlikely . . . "

"You don't want me to make a statement?"

"Why would we? We know the couple that live there have been taken by men you can't describe. They were driven away in a white van of unknown make and registration. You aren't able to tell us anything we weren't already aware of. But if you happen to remember anything useful . . . "

"Well, you've got my address. If you want to contact me during the day I work in my father's bookshop, Bennett's, on rue Berthe."

"You can go the long way home, back up the steps. This is now a crime scene."

And then he added, with heavy sarcasm: "Thank you for your help."

II.

I made myself a simple meal that evening, but couldn't eat it. I drank a whole bottle of cheap red wine; the first mouthful was bitter and almost rancid, but the second glass had improved on the first, and by the third I wasn't thinking about the taste.

The events in the Passage des Abbesses would not stop replaying themselves over and over in my mind, but the alcohol helped me sleep. When I woke up the next morning, a minute or so before the alarm was due to go off, I knew I'd been dreaming of the abduction. I'd been watching the whole thing from a different viewpoint, though, closer than in reality. The men were carrying ugly, heavy guns, and the naked man was screaming, although there had been tape over his mouth in reality. He had coarse black hairs over his emaciated body. The woman had terror in her eyes and she passed so close that I could have held out my hand to touch her.

Emerging from the dream I imagined striking out at the hooded man, landing a blow on his chin. In the scenario I created, the gun was dropped and I picked it up. I called out to them to put up their hands, and I shot at the tyres to stop the van from driving away . . .

As I lay in my comfortable bed, the early morning light finding its way around the curtains, I thought of the man and woman who had been taken. I imagined them being held somewhere, tied up, while a ransom was negotiated. I felt guilty for thinking that they'd both looked so pathetic, and I tried not to think of them being beaten.

I remembered the man being picked up off the ground, and I realised that the assailant couldn't have been holding a gun.

And then the alarm went off. I tried to dismiss what I had seen. I was up and about my usual routines, taking a shower, making breakfast and feeding the fish in the large tank in the living room. It was wrong that everything should continue as normal, but when I left the apartment I couldn't make myself climb up the steps to the rue des Abbesses towards the Passage. Instead, I turned left along the narrow part of rue Véron and then right up the anonymous rue Germain Pilon. The pavements were slick with rain that had come down in the night, and the city did not look as picturesque as it usually did. It was in the early morning that I appreciated Paris most, when the streets were blocked by delivery vehicles, and people were hurrying to work. As it prepared itself for the day, before the tourists filled the city, I always felt that I was a legitimate part of it. Normally I treasured the atmosphere, but I was now feeling as though I had never really belonged.

My father knew that something was wrong immediately I had arrived at the shop. We sat in the office and he let me talk.

Putting the events into words again brought back the trembling. I felt stupid that I was unable to relate what had happened without becoming emotional. A few years before my father wouldn't have listened to me so sympathetically or without interruption. However, since moving to Paris he seemed to have mellowed.

When I had finished, he ran his fingers through his long, grey hair and nodded. He lit a cigarette and I waited for him to say something. Then he got up from his chair and patted me on the shoulder. Almost absent-mindedly, he asked:

"The man who'd been looking in the shop window . . . was he one of our regular customers?"

"He looked like he ought to be."

My father frowned. Before I could say anything he said:

"I know you're embarrassed by the shop. But I rely on British customers just as much as English-speaking Parisians. It doesn't matter whether they're tourists or ex-pats."

"But do you really need the Union Jack on the shop sign and stationery?"

"I suppose you think they're the last refuge of the scoundrel? No doubt you see yourself as 'cosmopolitan', rather than allied to any particular country?"

I couldn't answer him directly because the accusations were correct. I said:

"The man annoyed me because he was reinforcing a stereotype."

This all seemed to be beside the point, but perhaps there was nothing my father could have said in reply to my account of the abduction.

As the day slowly passed I thought about the man with the cane, and wondered if my attempt to live in Paris was an affectation of its own; I had only followed my father across the Channel because I couldn't stay in London with my mother after what had happened. I also had a newly acquired English degree but didn't know what I wanted to do with it. If I was lonely in Paris, then at least it was a challenge to live in another country. In London I'd have been resentful.

After work, habit directed me on my usual route home, towards the Passage des Abbesses. It felt strange going down the steps, alongside the tourists, only to discover that there was nothing at all to be seen in the square. It was busy and people passed by without even realising that it had been the scene of a crime. I wanted to ask them where they had been twenty-four hours before.

For several days I heard nothing of the abduction, and was happy for it to be that way. The shop was busy during the day, and in the evenings there was a week-long season of early Polanski films at the cinema on the rue Tholozé. For four nights my dreams moved away from the abduction and back to Corrina, but then, on the Monday morning, I saw the front page of *Le Figaro*.

My father passed me the newspaper reluctantly, uncertain of my reaction. Prominently displayed was the photograph that the policeman had shown me. I wasn't wearing my spectacles, but I could see, clearly enough, that the young couple were sitting together on the grass, grinning at the camera. Her lip and nose were pierced, while he had a number of studs in his ears. He was wearing a striped shirt and shorts, and she had on a white summer dress and there were clips in her bright pink hair. I hadn't noticed the details when I'd seen the photograph before, but it was certainly the same one. The opening paragraph of the report stated that the naked bodies of Stefan and Camille Martischewsky had been pulled out of the Seine the previous day. There were unconfirmed reports that they had been tortured before being shot. I could read no further.

The morning passed slowly, although I worked furiously, arranging, rearranging, and dusting sections of bookshelves. That afternoon I took my father's car to collect a few lots that we had won at an auction over the weekend. Although I had learned to drive in London, Paris traffic always seemed more aggressive, and it took all my concentration to navigate to and from the auction house, and not to add to the dents in the car. However, even when my thoughts were determinedly on driving, the word "tortured" kept repeating itself in my mind. I did everything I could not to think about it, but still the couple's faces appeared before me. I didn't see them as they were in the photograph, happy and with no idea of their fate, or even how they had looked naked, bound and thrown into the back of the van. Their faces were presented to me as they had been in my dream; close and staring into my eyes, asking for help.

It was just after two o'clock that night when I woke up from a nightmare in which they were tied to chairs in a dark, underground room. I watched something happening to them, but was relieved not to be able to remember quite what it was. I woke up sweating and ashamed, because in my dream I'd somehow been colluding in their torture. In my dream Corrina was there as well.

Television provided a balm that night. Sitting in the living room I tried to watch an inane series of late-night programmes. I didn't want to go back to sleep, but frequently succumbed to fitful dozing.

III.

The parcel that had been delivered to the shop was well-wrapped. Under the brown paper was cardboard, a layer of bubble-wrap, and then plain white paper enfolding each of the individual Puffin books. They had been ordered for a customer, and I was preoccupied with checking them against the invoice when someone came in through the door.

I looked up and said "*Bonjour*", taking in the man's slightly square features and manicured appearance before I realised where I had seen him before.

"Good morning," he replied in English. "Do you, by any chance, sell Octavo Society books?"

"Reluctantly, yes."

"Why reluctantly?

"Well, we have a preference for first editions."

"I don't understand? I mean, the Octavo Society have only ever published classics, and they're beautifully designed. How can you fault them?"

"I can't, but their books will always be reprints, albeit very nice ones . . . " It seemed obvious that this was not the real reason for his visit. "You were in the Passage des Abbesses last week, when the abduction occurred."

He casually fixed my eyes with his own. The irises were bright blue, though the whites were unpleasantly yellowed and slightly bloodshot:

"Yes, and you were there too."

"But you walked away. I had to call the police."

"That was very public-spirited of you."

"I couldn't be of much help to them. I couldn't identify the people with balaclavas, or the van. But I know the police would like to talk to other witnesses, like you."

"I'm sure they would. But I'd only be able to give them the same information as you. We were both some distance away after all, and I expect your eyesight is better than mine."

"You really ought to go to the police. I told them there was another witness. I gave them your description."

"Did you? Well, I'm sure they'll have more important things to do than look for me."

I was angry with him: "The people who were taken that day were tortured before they were murdered. Their bodies were found floating in the Seine. Don't you read the newspapers?"

"That really is very unfortunate. It's probably all the more reason why we should both stay out of it. I mean, there are things that go on under the surface of any city . . . " His tone was measured and his words carefully chosen. He nodded gravely: "I admire your sense of duty."

After a pause he said, "My name is Reginald Hopper." He drew a card from out of an inside pocket and passed it to me. "I live on the rue St. Vincent. If you really feel the need to give my name to the police then please do so. I'd prefer it if you didn't, but the choice is yours. In the meantime, are you interested in selling me any books?"

"What are you after?"

"*The Bird Paintings of Henry Guthrie* by Bruce Campbell. It was published by the Octavo Society. It's their edition that I want, if that doesn't offend your sensibilities too much?"

"I don't think we have it."

"I thought it unlikely. It was limited to only five hundred copies. It's always eluded me for some reason."

My offer was made unwillingly: "We can undertake a search and let you know how much we'd charge. There'd be no commitment to buy."

"Thank you. But tell me why, exactly, you would favour a first edition over a Octavo Society reprint? Especially if the reprint is better designed, bound and illustrated."

I'd been working with my father long enough to have the answer ready:

"It's the thrill of finding a book exactly as the author and the public first saw it. It's how the publisher first issued it, after reading and liking the manuscript, probably with no idea whether it would be any kind of success."

I didn't want to be talking of books, but had to explain:

"If I'm to be honest, I don't like any institution that tells me what books I should be reading. I'd prefer to make the decision myself. People who collect just Octavo Society editions often do so with the idea that it implies they've got taste."

I was feeling belligerent.

"Well," he said with a smile. "I'm a Octavo Society *completist*."

"The world would be a dull place," I replied weakly, "if we all shared the same taste."

He laughed, repeated the title of the book he wanted, and left in apparent good humour. As the door closed behind him, my father appeared from the back of the shop.

"That's really quite extraordinary . . ." I started to say, staring at Hopper's card. "A man's just been in enquiring after a book . . ."

"So he was the other witness? I decided not to interrupt you; I could hear what you were saying."

"Yes, and he obviously doesn't give a damn about that poor couple!"

"That's up to him, I suppose. But I agree, it's odd." He took the card. "Reginald Hopper, eh?"

"Do you know him?"

"No, but I think he must be the man that Sebastian Bertrand, the *bouquiniste*, sells Octavo Society editions to. According to Bertrand, Hopper spends a lot of money. It'd be nice to pick him up as a customer. Bertrand met Hopper at some literary event and talked him into buying a whole lot of Octavo Society books that he hadn't been able to shift. *The Bird Paintings of Henry Guthrie*, eh? I'll make some enquiries."

I went back to the parcel of Puffin books and the door opened again. I took a couple of seconds before looking up with my usual "*Bonjour*". In that brief moment I identified the perfume and was sufficiently alert to recognise the woman who had entered.

"*Bonjour*," she said. "But you're English?"

"Yes, and so are you."

I was struck again by her resemblance to Corrina, but it was superficial; close up, and with the opportunity to appraise her properly, she appeared too fragile, and with dark-shadowed eyes. Her heavily made-up face was over-long, tapering to a small chin. She had a slight northern-English accent and was wearing the coat I had seen her in before. She was a shabby, cut-price Corrina and I despised her for it.

"It's a morning of coincidences," I said.

"Is it?"

"Last week, in the Passage des Abbesses, there was an abduction. I passed you on the steps just before it happened."

"Oh?"

"Well, you were probably too far away to see what happened. But our last customer was in the Passage at exactly the same time. I was standing right alongside him when it happened. By chance, he left here only a few minutes ago."

"I'm not sure it's really a coincidence," she said slowly. "You see, I know Reginald Hopper."

"I don't understand."

"Why was he here?"

"He wants us to find a book for him."

She considered this, and then said, "You called the police about the abduction?"

"Of course. It's what most people would've done, surely? Not that Hopper was interested. He just walked away."

"But you told the police what happened?"

"Yes."

"And did you tell them about Hopper?"

"I said there was another witness, but I didn't have his name then."

"Now you know who he is, you must tell the police."

"Why's it of any interest to you?" Even without her mocking resemblance to Corrina she would have started to irritate me.

"I know Hopper, and I think they should be told he was there, in the Passage, when it happened."

"He gave me his card, so I assume he's got nothing to hide."

She laughed unconvincingly. Her hands had been moving restlessly as we spoke and she now clasped them to her chest. They were long and elegant, but the fingernails were badly-bitten.

I asked, "Would *you* be prepared to give a statement?"

"I didn't see anything. As you said, I was too far away."

"But I saw you running up the steps. You must have known that something had gone on."

"I was just getting out of the way of Hopper."

"Why?"

"That's my business. Please, tell the police that he was there."

"That's not good enough," I said, and slowly walked around the counter. I wasn't going to physically prevent her from going out of the door, but I'd have liked to make it hard for her to leave without explaining herself. However, she had already started to back away.

"Look," I said. "I saw two people being violently abducted. It was horrible. And they've since been found dead. I don't mind admitting that I've had nightmares about the whole thing."

I tried moving forward again, but she retreated once more. Her hands were moving, uncertain whether to reach for the door, or perhaps be ready to push me away.

"Why don't we both go to the police?" I said. "I mean, if it's so important to tell them Hopper was there."

"No," she said. "I have reasons, good reasons."

"But we're talking about murder! If you have information *you* are the one who should be making a statement."

"There are reasons why I can't."

"If I should tell them about him, perhaps I should also tell them about you?"

"But I've not told you my name."

"If you want me to believe that he had something to do with it . . . "

As she moved towards the door it opened and Mrs. Travers entered. The younger woman had to step aside and Mrs. Travers looked at the two of us suspiciously before asking, "Have my Puffins come in?" She was a large woman with an upper-class accent, and I always found her intimidating.

"They've just arrived."

The young woman in the black coat took the opportunity to slip out of the door. I had to find the courage to say to Mrs. Travers, "Excuse me a moment."

Outside, I could see her walking quickly away up the narrow street.

"Hey, I *will* tell them about you!" I called.

She stopped and turned around unwillingly.

"I'd rather you didn't." Her eyes were large and pleading. "Tell them about Hopper, and I'll come and explain it all to you another time. Please. I promise I *will* explain."

IV.

Parisian officialdom of any sort has always worried me; there never seems to be any sincerity in the allowances they have to make for a foreigner. The policeman who took Hopper's card from me that afternoon at the *commissariat* made a note and promised to pass it on to the investigating officer. He smiled blandly and returned to his paperwork. I would have told him about the woman as well; I certainly hadn't fallen for the pathetic look in her eyes. But the man gave me the impression that I was wasting his time.

I returned to the shop to find it empty of customers, and my father sitting at the counter reading the newspaper.

"You told them all about Mr. Hopper?" he asked.

"Yes, but they didn't seem to care."

"I suppose he was right. If he was standing next to you he wouldn't have seen any more than you did."

"Perhaps."

"But I expect they'll follow it up. They have procedures; they'll need to cover themselves. It is a murder investigation, after all."

"That's what I thought, but I was made to feel like I was wasting their time."

"That young woman who came into the shop after him . . . "

"What about her?"

"I only saw her through the office door, but I'd been trying to think who she reminded me of. It's your Corrina . . . "

"We agreed that we wouldn't mention Corrina."

"We did," he said, and sighed before saying, 'Well, my news is that I've tracked down two copies of *The Bird Paintings of Henry Guthrie*. It's an odd book, published in association with the Zoological Society of London in 1976. Walter Hudson has a fine copy for a couple of hundred pounds."

"For a Octavo Society edition? Blimey."

"There were only five hundred copies printed. It seems to've been a first edition in its own right, rather than one of their reprints."

I yawned and my father said: "Why don't you knock off now. Go home and try and get a decent night's sleep without the aid of alcohol."

I decided to take advantage of his suggestion. Out of habit, when I left the shop I glanced up and down the road in case there were any potential customers. Instead, I recognised the young woman with the long black coat. She had turned away, but not quite quick enough. It was amusing to think of her as an elongated caricature of the old women in black who could still be seen on the Paris streets, apparently oblivious to the modern world around them.

I considered going after her, but then decided to see if she was following me. I did not turn left as usual at rue Androuet, but continued down to the Place Emile Goudeau and made my way through the pigeons and cigarette ends. I sat down on one of the green-painted benches under the trees, purposely choosing one that faced back towards the rue Berthe. There was still some warmth in the sun and I made myself comfortable and waited. Sure enough, some moments later, she appeared.

The woman glanced around and didn't notice where I was sitting until it was too late to hide. We made eye contact for less than a second before she broke it, looking exaggeratedly away. Her hands had leapt into the air, though, signalling her exasperation.

"Good evening," I called, hoping my grin would provoke her.

Reluctantly she came over.

"You're not very good at following people," I said.

"It's what I do. You've not noticed me before." Her hands were now determinedly clasped together. "You take the same route home from the shop to your apartment every night."

"Is that not allowed?"

She didn't answer.

"So, you've been stalking me?" I asked.

"I'm not really interested in *you*."

"Who are you interested in then?"

"I'd rather not talk out here."

She nodded in the direction of the café behind me.

"But why not here?" I asked. "It's pretty, under the trees. Did you know this area was once called Le Bateau-Lavoir?"

"I'm not interested in history."

"Famous artists lived here."

"Although following people is what I do," she said, ignoring my remarks, "sometimes people follow *me*. I don't want us to be overheard."

"You sound paranoid."

"I've reason to be."

"Okay then," I agreed, amused.

There were customers at the tables outside the café, but inside it was empty. Anodyne pop music was playing quietly from somewhere behind the bar and the place smelt of cleaning fluid and coffee. The woman selected a small, two-person table towards the rear, and when we were sitting opposite each other she started to explain:

"I follow Hopper."

"Why?"

"Because he's not what he claims to be."

"Which is?"

"He says he's a businessman and a philanthropist. He invests in small businesses, allowing them to expand, taking a share in the profits, sometimes selling them on."

"And what's wrong with any of that?"

"I'm aware of his history."

A large man with a startling beard, presumably the Patron, passed our table and wished us a good evening. We asked for two glasses of merlot, and the woman refused to explain anything until we had been served. She still reminded me of Corrina, and I wondered what I'd have been doing at that very moment if she had still been alive. I wondered whether we would still be living in London, and whether we would have finally moved in together.

Thoughts of what I had lost made me all the more aggravated by the woman sitting opposite me, and I derived some enjoyment from her nervousness and awkwardness. While we waited, she didn't know what to do with her hands; she either tapped them on the table or played with her thick black hair. She seemed relieved when she finally had a glass to hold.

"Hopper's a nasty piece of work," she continued. "His life is a front, a charade so that he can launder a large amount of gold bullion he got his hands on several years ago. He obtained it through violence; people died."

She was wearing red lipstick that was too bright for her pale complexion. When she took a gulp of wine it smeared the edge of the glass.

"Why don't you go to the police?" I asked.

"Because he went to court for it, back in England. It was a few years ago. He was tried and found not guilty."

"But you're sure he *is* guilty?"

"He claimed amnesia because of something that happened and he didn't plead either guilty or not guilty." She sipped her wine once more and then frowned, staring down at the glass rather than at me. "The court couldn't decide whether he'd stolen the gold and killed his accomplices, so he left court a free man. He started a new life over here in Paris, without knowing a word of French, and discovered that he could make money out of thin air; out of stupid little businesses. He's slowly turning the gold into clean cash."

She drank more of her wine and I realised I had not started mine.

"So, he may be a crook," I shrugged. "Thanks for the advice; I'll keep my distance."

"But he's very dangerous. What do you think he was doing in the Passage des Abbesses that evening?"

"You tell me."

"He was making sure his people carried out his orders."

"Oh?"

"It was his first serious mistake."

"Where's your information from?"

"I was a witness to what went on back in England. I've seen exactly what he's capable of."

"And you're here, in Paris, because of him?"

"I followed him for my own reasons, but there are others who're interested in Hopper and what he does. I'm employed by them to follow him when he's in Paris. I note down where he goes and who he talks to."

"Who are the people you work for?"

"I can't tell you that."

"Why should I listen to what you say, and take you seriously, when you won't tell me . . . "

"It's probably the French police, or some secret service. I don't actually know who they are. The person I speak to sounds English."

"Oh."

"I report to them and they pay me, in cash. Because you've been in contact with Hopper they're now interested in you."

"I really have nothing to do with Hopper."

"I told them that was probably the case."

"So why're you still bothering to follow me?"

"Because I think you might be able to give me information about him."

"For you to pass on to your employers? Not if you can't tell me who they are."

"It's personally very important to me as well."

"But you haven't even told me your name."

She put out her hand: "It's Candy Smith."

I decided not to take her hand, not yet: "Why should I believe your story? It's all quite unlikely. I mean you don't even know who's paying you!"

"I'm telling you all this because I think you've got a sense of right and wrong. You've talked to the police twice already."

As she spoke I was watching her impressive eyelashes moving, and realised that they were false. The Patron moved in our direction with a smile. He had noticed that Candy had emptied her glass.

"*Un nouveau verre pour Mademoiselle?*"

"*Non*," she said, standing up, not looking at the man. To me she said, "Trust me, I'm right. See what you can find out and then tell me."

The Patron and I both watched Candy leave.

"*Femme?*" said the man, wrongly concluding that there had been an argument. He raised his eyebrows, hoping for information.

I shrugged and sipped at my wine, leaving him to walk back to the bar, stroking his beard. When I left a few minutes later I could hear him saying to another customer "*Touristes!*"

Hopper returned to the shop a week later. I happened to glance up and see him through the window and I was able to slip into the office before he came in. My father had to serve him.

"You've found *The Bird Paintings of Henry Guthrie* for me?"

"Yes, it's under the counter," my father said proudly.

"So the younger gentleman was happy for you to handle it?" he asked with sarcasm.

"My son? Yes, well, it's actually a first edition in its own right."

"That's all right then," he mocked.

"I do share some of Flavian's misgivings about the Octavo Society, but this is a very interesting volume."

"Your son didn't convince me to give them up."

"Well, there's nothing intrinsically wrong with the Octavo Society. It's only when you compare some of their titles with the alternatives."

I didn't catch the reply. I could tell that my father had left the desk and he returned a few moments later.

"Tell me what you think of these . . . " he said. "We normally only sell English language editions, but I recently bought a first edition of this book in French. I already had the first American translation here, the first English translation, and this newer small press edition. Now . . . here's a Octavo Society edition I keep hidden from my son."

My father was showing Hopper copies of Alain-Fournier's *Le Grand Meaulnes*. He had always had a soft spot for the book:

"There's nothing wrong with the Octavo Society translation, although I prefer this later British edition. But tell me, which would you prefer, if given the choice and money was no consideration."

I could imagine Hopper picking up the different editions and putting them down again. While he did so my father asked if he had the Octavo Society edition already.

"Yes, I probably have."

"I promise you that the lithographs spoil the story."

There was more silence, and finally the man said:

"I'd be tempted by all of them, if I'm to be honest. I suppose the best translation would be the ideal one."

"That's the right answer!" said my father.

"I like this American edition as it looks almost new. Condition is very important to me. How much is this first edition?"

"Seven thousand euro."

"Really?"

"Yes."

"Well, I'll take the American edition, and this British one, if you recommend it. As long as we are not talking thousands of euro?"

"The two together would be three hundred."

"And so I owe you five hundred . . . I'll write you a cheque, if I may."

A few second later I could hear the man casually asking:

"I don't suppose you've ever come across a book called *The Dark Return of Time*?"

"It sounds familiar. I'll ask my son if he knows."

I was resigned to what would happen next. A moment later my father's head was around the side of the office door. "Have you heard of a book called *The Dark Return of Time*? I was thinking that Javier Marias was the author."

"No."

I knew that I couldn't hide any longer.

"Good morning," I greeted Hopper, and the man nodded and smiled in return. He was dressed very formally, as
usual, with a sky-blue waistcoat under his well-cut jacket.
He was immaculately groomed, but once again I was fasci-
nated by his eyes, which did not seem at all healthy.

"My father's thinking of *The Dark* Backward *of Time*,"
I said.

"No, that's not it. I don't actually know who the author is."

"We can look it up for you. We can search the online da-
tabases and if nothing comes up we can always advertise."

Hopper was unsure: "I think that, at the moment, I'd
like a little discretion."

"What's the problem?" I asked.

"I believe I can trust you both?"

"Of course," said my father, slightly offended.

"Well, it has no real value to anybody except me. If it's
on the shelves of a bookshop nobody could charge more
than ten pounds for it. But it does seem to be unaccount-
ably scarce. Between you and me I'd be happy to pay a
hundred, perhaps more."

"What category is it?"

"Biography, I think. It's very hard to tell."

"We'll see what we can do," my father said.

"Thank you," he replied with a benign smile, and then
he was looking directly at me and my heart started to
pound. "While I'm here, I'd like to talk to you?"

"Of course," I said, faltering.

Hopper was still smiling, but his eyes flicked unmistake-
ably to the office door. "In private, perhaps?"

"I don't have any secrets from my father," I said.

"Very well. It's with regard to Candy Smith."

"Oh . . . "

"You had a long talk with her a few days ago."

"Yes, er . . . "

"You really mustn't believe the half of what poor Candy says. You see, she's a little confused, poor dear. A little, shall we say, 'damaged'?"

"She did say some strange things."

I immediately regretted my words.

"Of course, I'm not aware of exactly how much she told you, but she has caused me some trouble in the past. Actually, a great deal of trouble. So I keep her busy; I pay her to keep an eye on my movements, and those of people around me."

"Why are you telling me this?"

"Because she'll have made some wild and unfortunate accusations that'll have worried you. But I don't want her to realise that we've spoken about her. That wouldn't be fair. I mean, none of this is fair really. Perhaps she ought to be in a hospital, but I make sure she has enough money to get by, and something to occupy her time. I can trust you not to say anything to her?"

"She said that she wanted me to spy on you as well."

He continued to smile the same fixed smile: "Perhaps I shouldn't be playing these games, but Candy needs to be busy, occupied, and believing she's doing some good."

"I'm not sure that I want to get involved in your games."

"I understand. It's your decision. But please don't mention this discussion to her; I don't think it would help her state of mind."

"Okay."

"It's nothing to do with me," my father said.

"Good."

Although the smile had disappeared, Hopper looked more at ease. He tapped his nose to suggest that it would all be kept a secret between us. He left the shop with his parcel of books and an air of satisfaction.

"That's a rum old set-up," my father commented. "But so long as he keeps asking for books, and writing cheques, I'll go along with it."

"None of it is right," I insisted. "Candy said she didn't know who was paying her to spy on Hopper. Would he really arrange all this just to keep her busy and out of his hair?"

"I suppose if he's rich enough . . . Maybe it makes him feel important?"

"It's not very fair on her, though. If she needs to be in hospital then perhaps that'd be the best place for her."

At that moment the door opened and Candy entered the shop.

"Hello," I said, guiltily.

"Can we talk?" she asked.

My father immediately said, "I'll go into the office." He shut the door after him.

"Why was Hopper here?" she demanded.

"He came to buy some books."

"Which books?"

"Is it important?"

"I'm not sure. It might be."

"I ought to respect client confidentiality."

"You're not a doctor, or a priest!"

"Okay. Will it help if I say he left with a couple of different editions of *Le Grand Meaulnes*, and an illustrated book about birds?"

She looked around nervously, playing with the ends of her hair.

"And there was nothing else?"

"Like what? He didn't tell us where the gold bullion was hidden."

She took a step back: "I thought I could trust you. Now you're just laughing at me."

"I'm sorry. But I don't understand what's going on."

"Well, perhaps I'll come back another time."

I was pleased to see her leave. As she was closing the door after her, though, she turned, remembering to thank me. I thought for a moment she was going to ask further questions, or give more of an explanation. I didn't encourage her, and finally, awkwardly, she left.

In the office my father looked up from his computer.

"I really don't know what to make of all this," I said.

"You didn't tell her that it's Hopper who's paying her to spy on him?"

"No. It's none of my business, is it?"

"I suppose not."

"I'm not happy with both of them hanging around. Whatever's going on between them I'm convinced that it's linked to that abduction. Candy's sure he's got something to do with it."

"And you believe her?"

"No, but it's too much of a coincidence. On the day that I witness a violent crime I also come across two people who act very strangely and make accusations against each other. I'm not sure what to do."

"Do nothing, for the moment. I mean, what could you tell the police?" He coughed. "Now, I think we might be able to steer your Mr. Hopper away from the Octavo Society."

"He's not *my* Mr. Hopper."

"We should move him towards collecting some more interesting books. We do have a living to make here . . . "

"I know, I know. But I'm not sure that we ought to be dealing with him at all."

"Nonsense. His money's as good as the next customer's."

"But if Candy's right about where he got it from."

"Are we going to turn down business because of a madwoman's story?"

"No . . . "

"While you were talking to her, I was searching for *The Dark Return of Time* on the 'net. It's odd, but there isn't a copy for sale anywhere, and it doesn't turn up on the British Library catalogue, the Library of Congress website or the Biblioteque Nationale."

V.

Hopper's large, ostentatious house on the south side of rue St. Vincent was built hard up against the road, next to a small and incongruous vineyard. The ground floor windows were shuttered and the front door looked medieval, apparently constructed out of heavy oak planks with primitive wrought metalwork. The intercom was state-of-the-art, though, and when my father pressed the button the response was almost instantaneous. He gave his name and business, and the door opened a moment later.

A bald man in an ill-fitting suit stared at me suspiciously and asked who I was. My father explained, although he did not admit, naturally, that I had tried to dissuade him from personally delivering the copy of *Le Grand Meaulnes*.

"He can come and collect it from the shop," I had said.

"When a customer is paying seven thousand euro for a book, the personal touch is required." I was made to feel ten years old again. "It didn't take much to persuade Hopper that he wanted the first edition. He'll be our best customer if he's happy to spend so much money so easily."

We followed the man, whose skull was craggy under the white skin, and whose blue veins stuck out randomly, almost threateningly. He tapped sharply on a door and opened it without waiting for a response. Hopper was sitting behind a desk at the far end of a long, well-lit room filled with bookshelves.

"Gentlemen," he beamed at us, screwing the lid on his fountain pen. "Do come over here. You're bearing treasure, I hope."

Hopper was formally dressed, as usual, this time with a canary-yellow waistcoat under a silver-grey jacket. He matched his room, which was immaculate, although the polished wooden shelves were only half full of books. I noted the ostentatious "antiqued" globe and the library steps.

"*Le Grand Meaulnes*," my father announced. "Published by Emile-Paul Frères here in Paris in 1913. The original run was only a thousand copies. Not many have survived in this condition."

He reverentially handed the bubble-wrapped package over to Hopper while I browsed the man's books. I had decided that Hopper was a philistine, but from the corner of my eye I saw him remove the copy of *Le Grand Meaulnes* from its protection with the proper reverence.

"I wasn't terribly well-educated," Hopper explained to my father. "I didn't have any interest in books as I grew up. And then in my thirties I had time to read during a long spell in hospital. That was due to your son's friend, Candy. While recuperating I discovered what I'd been missing. Since then I've been educating myself. I've an ambition to create the perfect library. I hope that you might be able to help me."

"We'd be very pleased to," said my father with what I recognised as some satisfaction. He, too had dressed up for the occasion, and for the first time ever I had seen him run a comb through his unkempt hair.

I couldn't help saying, "I'm not sure that the perfect library can ever be created."

"For the individual, I'm sure it can be," said my father. He was pronouncing his words with a little more care than usual, affecting a cultured tone in competition with his host. "It depends on their personal preferences, of course . . . So, what books, Mr. Hopper, really appeal to you?"

"As I say, I'm not an educated man. I'm open to recommendations."

"Well, it would be useful if you could tell us what you've liked in the past. Do you enjoy traditional storytelling, as in *Le Grand Meaulnes*, or would you prefer something more modernist, *avante garde* and experimental like James Joyce?"

"I've not read Joyce. I suppose that I should."

"Perhaps not just yet . . . Have you ever read Dickens?"

My father continued to try and define the man's interest in literature. While I was less than impressed with Hopper's taste, I must admit that I was surprised by his huge collection of Octavo Society books. There were the usual common titles, but also a facsimile edition of Dr. Johnson's *Dictionary of the English Language* printed by the St. Edmundsbury Press on lovely paper, bound in leather. Next to it was a brand new but magnificent *Canterbury Tales* illustrated by Eric Gill. I had seen the original many years ago at a book fair, but this was a handsome edition. The book I picked off the shelf after that was a beautiful anniversary edition of *Don Quixote* by Cervantes. I had to get my glasses out to inspect it properly.

Hopper was saying, " . . . well, if I am to move away from the Octavo Society I don't just need recommendations, I'll need a librarian."

He looked at me and waved his hand towards his shelves, "Should I consign all of these to the dustbin then?"

"No," I admitted, grudgingly. "Some of these are all right."

Hopper seemed pleased by my reaction and continued to write my father a cheque. As he handed it over he asked, "So, what made you open an English language bookshop in Paris?"

My father smiled and asked, "Why not?" He wasn't going to admit that he had split up with my mother ten years before and felt it best to put distance between them. In turn, he asked Hopper, "What brought you here?"

"I thought that I could escape, but it hasn't really worked like that. Already an old associate has come to work for me."

"And Candy?" I asked.

"She followed me too, and is a constant reminder of a past I can't even remember."

I was going to ask him to elaborate, when Hopper asked:

"So, would you like to work as my librarian?"

"I'm not really qualified."

"I don't want a *qualified* librarian. I want somebody who knows literature. If you could give me a couple of hours each week, as long as you can be spared from the shop . . . "

"He'd be happy to," my father agreed.

"Good. I'll pay you a hundred euro in cash for a couple of hours on, say, Friday mornings. And between you and your father, I'm sure you can elevate the status of my library. We'll decide what I need and if you let me see your receipts I'll pay you 120% of them."

"We have a deal," my father beamed, putting out his hand.

"I haven't agreed," I pointed out. "Are you sure I'm not just an affectation, like the globe and those wingback chairs?"

"Let me remind you who's paying your wages," said my father, and I came close to reminding him that he wasn't paying me very much. He turned back to Hopper and said, "We are still searching for a copy of *The Dark Return of Time* for you."

"There's no rush; I've been looking for a while . . . "

"Well, there're no copies in the big, international libraries. There are none offered online, and no records of copies sold at auction. I even searched the new titles database. When do you think it was published?"

"Ten years ago? Perhaps less."

"Was it a private publication, do you think?"

"It's possible. Please do keep searching, but in the meantime, what should I read next?"

"*The Horse's Mouth*, by Joyce Cary," I said, my eye having just seen the title on the shelf.

"Any particular reason?"

"It's a very good book," I said. It would be a test of the man's taste.

I only walked a part of the way back to my father's shop with him. I decided to take the afternoon off rather than continue the argument we were having about me working as Hopper's librarian.

Hopper phoned my father to say that he had finished reading *The Horse's Mouth*. He explained that it had taken some time to understand what was going on in the novel, but thereafter he had been gripped by it. He asked us to obtain a first edition for him.

When my father replaced the handset he complained, "It's a shame you didn't suggest he read his *Collected Sherlock Holmes* set. Just imagine the commission we'd be earning, buying those as first editions for him! Still, I suppose we can't ask him to spend thousands of euro every time."

"A library ought to reflect the personality of the person who's put it together."

"Mr. Hopper's library doesn't do that *yet* . . . "

"And it never will; not if we're directing him. It'll be a sham, assembled for show."

"That's a bit harsh. I think he genuinely wants the best possible books on his shelves."

"Books as furniture?"

"Now, that is unfair. He's actually reading the books we suggest. You're not jealous?"

"I suppose I am. But our lives are reflected in the books we have around us. They're a record of who we are, where we've been and what we've achieved."

"Perhaps we should think of Hopper as only now setting out on that voyage?"

We had been discussing shutting the shop early and it now seemed like a good decision. During the week following the argument with my father, we had managed to move on, and neither of us wanted to restart it.

I took my accustomed route home, thinking about my future, and whether I wanted to go back to England. It had been a glorious day and the light was softening as it started to cool. In the small square in the Passage des Abbesses I stood in the doorway from which Hopper had watched the abduction.

The shock of what had happened there was starting to fade. There was a strong smell from the drains that I'd not noticed before, and a couple of workmen were looking around as if trying to trace the source. Once more it seemed wrong that the world carried on just as before, when it had ended so horribly for those two people. I reasoned that it was nothing more than coincidence that my life had intersected with theirs; it had been pure chance that had enabled me to glimpse a scene in which I had no part to play.

Standing in the doorway, Candy's explanation of why Hopper had been there seemed far-fetched to me, but not impossible. Having met him a few times I didn't really want to believe her. Although I still thought his book collection pretentious, he had generally acted with humility, allowing himself to be lectured to and directed by me and my father. That he was using us I had no doubt, but it was a business arrangement that benefitted both parties.

I was pondering this when Candy turned up. I usually looked out for her as I went around the city, but had not noticed her following me for a day or two. We saw each other at the same time and she was resigned to having been discovered.

"Hello," I greeted her. "Following me again?"

"So what if I am?"

Something about her manner suggested that she might have been drinking.

"Candy, if you want to know where I'm going and what I'm doing you only have to ask."

"Have you seen Hopper since last week? You and your father took a parcel around to him."

"No."

"What was in the parcel?"

"A book. He did phone us this afternoon, though, to order another one."

"What were they?"

"*Le Grand Meaulnes* by Alain-Fournier and *The Horse's Mouth*, by Joyce Cary."

"When you went around to his house, did you see anything untoward?"

"Like what?"

"Handley answered the door?"

"Some man did. I wasn't told his name."

"He was English?"

"Yes. He was bald."

"That would be Handley. He's a nasty piece of work."

"He wasn't exactly friendly."

A group of students were moving towards us and while we waited for them to pass she sighed and leant against the wall as though tired. She closed her eyes for a moment; her false eyelashes were like damaged spiders. Forcing herself upright, she said,

"Hopper lets Handley get his hands dirty on his behalf. I did wonder if Handley was one of the men in balaclavas you saw."

"I wouldn't know. Have you been drinking?"

"So what if I have?"

"It's just that you don't look well. Where do you live?"

"What's it to you?"

"It seems to me that you need to go home, to bed."

"I'm fine."

"No you're not. Why don't I walk you home and you can ask me questions as we go?"

I knew I was acting out of pity, but I offered her my arm and she took it reluctantly.

"I haven't drunk that much," she insisted. "Have you heard anything from the police? They haven't said anything to you about Hopper?"

"They've not been in contact."

"It's likely Hopper's got people on the inside."

"That sounds a bit fanciful."

"Does it?" As we passed it, she nodded meaningfully at the door out of which the couple had been taken.

"A few months ago I saw Hopper and Handley both going through that door. They're connected with the people who lived there."

"I didn't know that."

"Well, you wouldn't have done. There are lots of things you don't know."

"Would you like to tell me some of them?"

"Perhaps, when the time is right."

At the rue des Abbesses we walked down past the busy restaurants and bars towards the Metro. I had a horrible presentiment that she was going to take us down under the Guimard canopy, and I wondered how far I was going to have to travel with her to see her home. She continued on, though, in silence.

After another few hundred yards I asked, "So, Hopper and you have a past?"

"Did he say that?"

"Intuition," I replied, as casually as I could.

"Yes, we do."

"Is that one of the things you want to tell me?"

"Perhaps."

She stopped suddenly, and because she was holding my arm I wheeled around. She buried her head in my chest and clung to me. Passers-by looked at us suspiciously as she sobbed, and I held her carefully, trying to stay calm. A large man in overalls stopped and watched us, presumably waiting to see if he could offer Candy assistance.

After a few moments she composed herself and asked if we could go on.

"I promise I *will* explain," she said, holding my hand, like we were a couple. It felt uncomfortable; there seemed to be dozens of people watching us, but I didn't say anything.

In the rue des Martyrs we turned left into a quiet cul-de-sac; rue André Gill. It was quite well-to-do, with the entrance to a hotel at the end, but Candy stopped at a plain wooden door covered in graffiti. It took a few moments for her to feel in various pockets for her keys. When the door was finally opened there was an exhalation of dampness from the dark interior.

"Are you all right from here?" I asked. She looked nervous.

"When I came home last night, I was sure somebody'd been in my rooms."

"Was anything stolen?"

"No, none of my stuff's worth stealing, but someone's been going through it."

My heart sank, but I offered to go up with her, to make sure she was all right. She nodded, pathetically, and I followed her up four flights of stairs which became progressively more narrow.

Candy's rooms were even smaller than mine. They were also a good deal more squalid, with a few pieces of old, uncomfortable furniture, and curling linoleum on all of the floors.

"It's a bit of a shit-hole," she said, as if noticing for the first time. "But it's all I can pay for. Your bookshop must be doing well if you can afford an apartment on the rue André Antoine."

"I'm staying there through a friend of my father. It's on the understanding that I feed a large aquarium of tropical fish."

"Lucky you."

"I still have to keep up with the day-to-day bills. My father can't pay me properly for working with him, so it's a good arrangement."

She sat down in the one armchair in the main room and put her head in her hands.

"Shall I make you a coffee?" I asked. The area partitioned-off as a kitchen was very old-fashioned, with a large, stained ceramic sink and a wooden draining board. A few items of crockery were on an open shelf with a packet of coffee and very little else.

Candy said, "No. I think I need something alcoholic."

"Are you sure you should have any more to drink?"

"I haven't got any, anyway. I haven't got any more money until I'm paid next."

"Oh."

I looked down at her, sitting there in her thin clothes, in the run-down apartment, and was angry with Hopper for keeping her in this state.

"So, what happened between you and him?" I asked.

She took a deep breath and sat back in her chair.

"Ten years ago I tried to kill him," she said, pulling a lump of stuffing out of a hole in the arm of the armchair

"Oh."

"Yeah, 'Oh'! I put a handgun up under his chin and pulled the trigger. Bang! Stuff shot out the top of his head . . . "

"And he survived?"

She nodded: "He has a tin plate in his skull."

"But the bullet would've gone through his brain!"

"It did. And it didn't do him much good. He was a year recuperating in hospital, and he came out a different person, *apparently*. They say his personality completely changed. And he claims he has amnesia; no memory of his past whatsoever."

"But you don't believe him?"

She shrugged, pulling out more stuffing and then picking it apart. "Who am I to say?"

"Didn't it get you into a lot of trouble?

"Yes. I got eighteen years for attempted murder."

"How long ago was that?"

"Ten years ago. It was horrible, but I was a good girl, and I was released on parole after nine years."

"You're not on the run then?"

"Well, no, but I'm not meant to be here, in Paris."

"Why did you try to kill him?"

She looked at me directly: "Because the bastard killed my father."

"I'm sorry," I said, and the words embarrassed me by their meaninglessness. "Was he convicted?"

"No."

"But he definitely did it?"

"I saw him do it. My father'd returned home from being abroad for a few days, or so I'd thought. I was going to run down the stairs to say hello, when I saw Hopper letting himself in through the back door. I saw him from the top of the stairs and knew something was wrong. He didn't see me, though. I heard them talking; I crept down and eavesdropped. And then, from my hiding place, I saw Hopper execute my father and leave."

Candy's eyes were focussed on the middle distance. She continued:

"I did what I thought was the right thing. I called the police and told them what happened. They picked Hopper up almost immediately."

She paused again and then asked, "Would you mind going out and buying some wine?"

"Are you sure?"

"I'm not going to be able to tell you any more unless I'm very pissed."

The door to Candy's building was shut when I returned. There was no bell or buzzer to contact her, and though I knocked loudly, several times, nobody came to answer it. From across the narrow street I looked up, but there was no sign of Candy at what I guessed were her windows. Frustrated, I shouted. My voice was loud in the cul-de-sac, but there was no response. A man in uniform came out of the hotel and stared at me, but didn't say anything.

I waited on Candy's doorstep for a half-hour, two bottles of wine on the pavement next to me. I knocked occasionally, but she still didn't answer. Exasperated, I finally walked out of the rue André Gill, and on the rue des Martyrs was nearly run into by a man on a bicycle freewheeling down the pavement. He shouted something at me which I didn't try to understand, partly because I was surprised at the size of the large dog sitting in the basket on the front of his bike.

In my own apartment I managed to drink one of the bottles of wine while watching a film on television, and I went into the bookshop the next day with a hangover. I wanted to tell my father how frustrated I was by Candy, but as I arrived he was leaving to view an auction in Saint-Quentin. I was meant to be reorganising a shelf of poetry books, and I was irritated that the first customer to arrive, not five minutes later, was Hopper.

"*The Horse's Mouth*," he said, launching into discussion in a friendly manner. "I got quite carried away with the style. Are Cary's other books the same?"

"I don't think so, but I've not read them," I said. "There's a series, all told from the other main characters' points of view."

"Ah, but not by Gimson?"

"No."

"Well, in that case, what do you recommend I read next?"

He was leaning on his cane and I couldn't stop myself from echoing my father's suggestion. "Why not read the Sherlock Holmes stories?" I said. "I saw you had a set."

"I'll read them next," he said, and asked, "How well do you know Candy Smith?"

"I don't, not really. Why?"

"Well, she called-in her report this morning and, among the other information she passed on, was that she'd been talking to you again."

"She'd been following me."

"But you went back to her apartment. She didn't follow you there."

I stopped working, "No. I walked her back to her apartment because she was unwell. Why?"

"I'm just interested. Tell me, what do you think of her?"

"That's none of your business."

"Do you find her attractive?"

"No." I tried not to sound annoyed.

"You're not sweethearts, then?"

The man was becoming impossible. I looked him in the eye, ready to tell him to go to hell. I think he sensed this.

"I'm sorry," he said with a wide smile. "I'm not meaning to tease you. I just wondered if something had happened; whether you'd argued."

"No, nothing happened. Look, I'm really not comfortable with all of this stupidity."

"It is actually quite serious."

"You're the one playing games."

"I have my reasons."

"Did she really tell you I'd been to her apartment?"

"No, actually. The information didn't come from Candy."

I considered this for a second.

"Bloody hell! Then you've got somebody else spying on the person you pay to spy on you? That's ludicrous. Either that, or you're spying on me as well."

"Did you talk to her?"

"It's got nothing to do with you!"

"Did she tell you that she once tried to kill me?"

"Yes, she did."

"Perhaps you'll understand now why I keep an eye on her. But you did draw attention to yourselves. All that hammering on her door and shouting in the street."

"This is unfair."

"In what way? Unfair to you or Candy?"

"To her."

"What else should I do? Call the police and tell them she's stalking me?"

"But you're paying her to stalk you!"

"I'm only paying her for what she'd be doing anyway. Did she tell you that by being here in France she's broken the terms of her parole? If the police knew, then she'd be extradited. She'd most likely end up back in prison."

"Maybe that would be a good thing? Then at least she might get some help; some counselling."

"I'm not sure if she's willing to see reason, even with the best medical help."

"Well, I don't think my father and I can do business with you."

He was shocked: "Really? That would be a shame. After all, if I enjoy those Sherlock Holmes stories I'll want the first editions."

"You're paying for our silence?"

"Of course not! But are they expensive, the first editions of the Sherlock Holmes stories?"

"Yes," I said, not knowing whether he knew that already.

"Well, I'll read them, and I'll tell you what I think. But for now I'll let you get on with your work. Mind you, I expect you'll receive another visitor once I've left. Candy was up and about early this morning. Perhaps she'll come by and ask what we were discussing. Then you can continue your talk from yesterday evening."

I was fuming, but I made myself resume re-shelving the books. A few minutes later I heard the door open again and I dreaded that Hopper's prediction would be correct. But the customer was not Candy. In fact, it was not until I had reopened the shop just after lunch that she arrived. She came inside hesitantly, looking around.

"Can we talk?" she asked.

"What, about Hopper?"

"Is there anybody else here?"

"No, just us."

"I'm, I'm frightened."

She appeared tired and dishevelled; she was wearing the same clothes as the day before and I wondered if she had changed them. At least she didn't seem to be drunk.

"Somebody came to my apartment yesterday evening," she said nervously, picking up a book and then putting it back down. "They were banging on my door, demanding to be let in."

"That was me! You sent me out to get some wine and when I got back the door was shut."

"And were you there doing the same thing this morning?"

"No."

"I don't know who it was, then. While they were banging on the front door, I went out the back. There's a yard for the bins . . . " she said trailing off, distracted. She drummed her fingers on the counter nervously. "I came straight here. I think they're after me."

She asked if I'd shut the shop so that we wouldn't be disturbed.

"Only if you tell me everything."

I turned the sign over and locked the door. In the office I made us both coffee while she sat and leafed through a book of Arthur Rackham's drawings, although she didn't really look at them. I noticed that her mascara was only a residual mess around her eyes and the false lashes had gone.

"Why aren't you more annoyed with me?" she asked.

"I *am* annoyed, but you remind me of an old girlfriend," I said, fully intending the reply to be ungallant.

"What was her name?"

"Corrina."

"Didn't it work out?"

"She died. There was a car accident, on an icy morning. It was nobody's fault."

"I'm sorry," she said gently.

"So am I," I said, regretting having said anything. "Last night you were telling me about Hopper. You saw him kill your father . . . "

"Yes," she said, and looked down at her hands and picked at her cuticles. Eventually she continued, "It was only my anger that stopped the grief from overwhelming me. Hopper was claiming to have nothing to do with my father's death. And there'd been a robbery; I told you about that?"

"You think Hopper's been laundering gold here in Paris."

She nodded.

"They said my father took part in the robbery, and that Hopper had nothing to do with it. They couldn't pin anything on him. He ran a small club in London and posed as a respectable businessman. He didn't even have a criminal record."

Candy started tapping her fingers against each other.

"It was hard enough coming to terms with my father's death. Accusing him of robbery was unbelievable, but then they accused him of having killed a security man! I didn't believe them; I couldn't. The only person I knew who was capable of murder was Hopper!

"I probably didn't make much sense to the police at first. I was confused and in shock. They tried getting me medical help for my *delusions*. For a while I refused to believe my father had been involved in anything, but then I discovered his gun. The police hadn't found it, but I guessed where to look.

"Having a gun didn't mean that he'd killed anyone, did it? It certainly didn't diminish what Hopper had done; what I'd seen him do . . .

"I was so angry and so frustrated that I went to Hopper's club one afternoon. The front door was open and unattended. I walked straight in to where he was sitting, talking with a couple of other men. They were at a table on a slightly raised platform. It was dark inside and they didn't notice me until I was standing there. I was able to put my arm out and the barrel of the gun up under Hopper's chin."

Candy was shaking as she spoke. I hadn't been looking at her face, but down at her ever-moving hands. She picked up her cup and I could see the surface of her coffee trembling. Then the spoon on her saucer started to rattle. I put my hand on her arm to try to calm her. She smiled at me weakly.

"Have you ever fired a gun?" she asked.

"No."

"It hurts."

"The recoil?"

"I was probably holding it at a stupid angle. When it went off it hurt my hand, and my wrist. I was looking at him as I pulled the trigger and the gun jumped out of my hand. The other men ran and I did the same. I didn't cover my tracks. I didn't think about anything like that. And I'd shot him in front of witnesses. They caught me easily enough. I didn't try to hide."

I took my hand away. For a moment I had felt protective of Candy, but what she had done scared me.

"You got eighteen years for attempted murder?"

"It was a confusing trial. They didn't believe why I'd shot him. There was no proof that Hopper had murdered my father. I was easy to convict, though. I tried to plead guilty on the understanding that I'd had good reason, but it doesn't work like that. My counsel wanted to say it was 'diminished responsibility', but I wouldn't let him. I ended up talking to psychiatrists who said there was nothing wrong with me. The judge refused to make any 'allowances'."

"Hopper was never tried?" I asked.

"A year later there was a hearing, of a sort, in front of a judge. Hopper had been in hospital, recuperating. Apparently his survival was a miracle; it was in all the newspapers. He didn't testify on his own behalf at the hearing; he said he couldn't plead guilty or not guilty because he knew nothing about anything before the shooting. Everyone thought this was wonderful of him. As if he had a choice, if he was telling the truth!"

Candy's hands were still shaking, but they had stopped moving around. She was looking at them herself.

"Apparently there was no proof of his involvement in the death of my father, or the theft of the gold and the killing of the security man. The evidence was all circumstantial. I was asked to give a statement, but it was discredited because of what I'd done. I really believe that the judge at the hearing let him go because he was said by all the doctors to be, in effect, a different person."

"You served your sentence, though."

"Half of it, because of good behaviour, cooperation, psychiatric reports . . . To start off with I protested, but then I realised that telling them I must've been mistaken, and that I was sorry, would get me out sooner. It stuck in my throat to say those things, but it's a game you have to play. And it makes *them* feel better."

"When you got out you weren't able to forget it, move on and start a new life?"

"No. I'm not sure I ever intended to. When I was released I was approached by a reporter called Dobson who was trying to dig stuff up on Hopper. It was he who told me that Hopper had moved to Paris and was finding it very easy to set up businesses and make money. The bullion had never been found and this reporter was convinced, but couldn't prove, that it was being laundered by Hopper.

"I came over here with him, just for a week, and after only a couple of days he disappeared. I've been here ever since, on my own."

"What can I say?" I needed time to turn her story over in my mind.

"Will you help me?" she asked.

"I don't know how to."

When I reflect upon what happened next I am ashamed. I decided that I wanted to help Candy, but there was nothing I could do to change what had happened in her past. I didn't know if I completely believed her story, but I was convinced that she was sincere.

I hugged her. When I tried to pull away she was unwilling to let me go. I brushed the hair from her face and kissed her lightly on the lips. I thought of Corrina and I suppose that my longing for her was a physical thing. I kissed her, and we continued to kiss until I noticed the tears running down her cheeks.

"I don't know why I'm crying," she said, and started to laugh. She still held me tight and when I tried to wipe away the tears she laughed all the more. She wouldn't let me go, though, and then she kissed me with more passion than before.

I responded willingly. Her body felt warm and hard against mine. My hands were inside her coat, under her shirt, as we continued to kiss and I ignored the sound of somebody trying to open the shop door. A few moments later we heard the key unlocking it; my father had returned.

Candy looked around rather wildly and insisted on leaving.

"Goodbye, Corrina," said my father, as she rushed past him

"Candy!" I insisted.

He flushed red, and corrected himself. Then he noted, "The shop was shut . . . I won't ask. Anyway, you'll never guess what I found at the auction at Brignole's . . . a copy of *The Dark Return of Time*! It's in an assorted lot of crime and non-fiction."

"So maybe it's not that rare after all?"

"Perhaps, but it's in a deplorable condition. I hardly dare tell Hopper. I don't know how desperate he is for a copy."

"Pretty desperate."

"But it's seriously tatty, torn and stained. It gives the impression of having been soaked in some horrible brown liquid and left outside. The other books in the lot aren't in great condition either."

"How much can you charge him?"

"Even if he wants it, not a lot; not in that condition. But no matter; I think that charging him exactly what we have to pay is the best course."

"He was in here earlier. I said I wasn't sure if we wanted his business."

"Because of that bedraggled girl? Well, *I* want his business and this is my shop. I hate to pull rank . . . "

"It's just that there's some stupid game going on, and I think she's the victim."

I explained what I had heard from both Hopper and Candy.

"And you're inclined to support her, are you?" my father asked. "She's obviously unstable. She's admitted to trying to kill him, and is here in France illegally. Whereas he's never been convicted of anything, and the only accusations come from her . . . "

"I realise how it looks."

"Well, as long as you understand, and as long as you don't lose me a good customer."

"Hopper asked what he should read next."

"As I'm doing him a great favour, I hope you suggested something expensive?"

"I took your advice and sent him in the direction of the Great Detective."

"Good lad!"

"Well, as I say, I'm not so sure I want anything to do with the man. And neither should you."

"The funny thing with regard to Hopper's book," my father said, "is that it has no author's name and no publisher's imprint. I reckon it's a vanity production."

"Did you get to read any of it?"

"To be quite honest, I didn't like handling it. But of course I had a quick look. He's right; it is some kind of biography. The subject's name isn't actually given, but I didn't much like what I read."

My father phoned Hopper, and a half an hour later he came through the door in an obviously serious mood. He made certain that there were no customers, and turned the sign to *fermé*.

"To business," he said. "You're sure it's the right book?"

"It's possible there's another with the same title," my father told him.

"But unlikely?"

"You really need to go to Brignole's yourself. If you get there before ten tomorrow you'll have a chance to inspect it before the sale."

"I shouldn't risk drawing attention to the book. Did you have a chance to read any of it?"

"No," my father lied.

Hopper rubbed his chin in that irritating way he had, while my father sat back and folded his arms. Not admitting that he had read any of the book made me wonder if my accusations and suspicions weren't worrying him after all. I was happy to cause trouble:

"You suggested before that you thought it was a biography?"

"Perhaps, yes."

"Your biography?"

"For all I know, maybe it is."

"You don't remember your own past, apparently," I said.

Hopper looked at me: "The actions of your friend Candy Smith saw to that."

"The main reason a biography might be anonymous," I said, thinking that I was being clever, "is because the author knew the subject would be unhappy with what they'd written."

Hopper raised his eyebrows, inviting me to go on, but I dried up.

He said, "Candy Smith was in here earlier, I take it?"

"Yes, she stopped by."

"I hope she has told you everything. And I mean *everything*."

"She has, yes."

"She told you what the professionals think of her stories, and the legal opinion."

"Yes."

He turned back to my father.

"I'll leave you to bid on this book for me."

"I'm happy to do so."

"I'd still like to be there, though, to make sure everything goes to plan. You said it's in a mixed lot?"

"Yes, with an estimate of three to four hundred euro. It's overvalued, if you ask me, considering the condition of the books."

"We'll have to work out a commission for you."

"I'm sure we can titivate a few of the other books, and sell them in time."

"It's a little premature to celebrate, but I'm having some friends around tomorrow evening for dinner and I'd like you two to join us."

"We couldn't intrude," said my father.

"Nonsense. I enjoy having company and I insist. I'll consider you both my guests of honour. Now, you are both single, aren't you? I'll have to arrange the seating plan, you see, and I'll make certain the rest of the party is congenial."

"I don't think I can," I said.

"Flavian . . . If I may call you Flavian? I imagine that because of what Candy's told you, you're wary of me.

Well, give me a chance to show you that I'm not the monster she's described. I'd like you and your father to think of me as a friend, as well as a customer. I'll be offended if you don't take up my invitation."

I said that I would think about it.

"Good! Then, you'll both be there at seven. Formal dress."

VI.

My father claimed to be unwell, but I didn't believe him. He was standing behind the counter with a handkerchief to his mouth, making ineffectual coughing noises. He explained that, of course, he could not possibly travel up to the auction in Saint-Quentin.

"So I have to go with Hopper?"

I was reminded of how he had once been with my mother; full of unbelievable excuses.

"Then he can go to the bloody auction on his own," I said.

"I hate to pull rank, but this is my business."

"I can always go back to England."

"That'd be a shame, of course. But perhaps you could make it up with your mother . . . She really wasn't to blame for Corrina's death . . . "

I refused to reply. In fact, I refused to talk to him all morning. I was meant to be mending a shelf in the office, but instead I read the newspaper until Hopper's Mercedes arrived. When it stopped at the door nobody appeared and I realised I was expected to go out to him.

Hopper and I sat together in the back of the car and there was an uncomfortable silence as we threaded our way out to the A1. Once we were travelling north past the Stade de France, he asked general questions about my mother and father. He enquired as to where we had lived in England, and where I had been to university. They were not unreasonable questions, they were friendly even, but I had no desire to be friendly.

"I'd ask after your past," I said, "but you've conveniently forgotten it."

"It's not that convenient," he replied, with a smile.

"People must have told you about your life?"

"Yes, and they tried to kick-start my memory. I've had many meetings with people I was supposed to've known; their stories meant nothing to me. Likewise, photos and mementoes were meaningless. Apparently I was brought up in South London, with three younger sisters, and though I was married my wife passed away a couple of years before I ever met Candy Smith. I ran a couple of nightclubs, quite successfully."

"You didn't want to keep on with that old life?"

"As far as I was concerned I was going to have to start again, no matter where I was or what I did. And I found that I didn't get on with the people I was meant to've known all my life. They said I'd changed, and how was I to argue with them? Selling up and starting again in Paris was easier."

"It must be odd not having memories of your childhood, your family, your wife."

"Perhaps, but you don't miss what you don't remember."

"Where did your start-up cash come from?"

"Selling my assets in the UK . . . My accounts have been thoroughly investigated by the authorities and are all above-board. You know, I've just started reading the Sherlock Holmes stories again . . . "

"Again?"

"Yes. When I first came over to Paris I was searching amongst the *bouquinistes* on the banks of the Seine and came across a man who sold detective fiction. It was trashy stuff mainly, but he persuaded me to buy the first of my

Octavo Society editions. Among them was the Sherlock Holmes set."

"So you'd read Doyle before?'

"You're convinced that I'm a complete philistine."

"No," I lied.

"You understand as well as I do that certain books become personal."

"And the book you're hoping to buy today?"

"The book I *will* buy today," he said, and smiled. "I'll tell you whether I'm admitting it to my collection when I finally get my hands on it."

Throughout the conversation I had been looking without much thought between the front seats, through the windscreen at the heavy traffic on the dull, busy road. Once we had left Paris the A1 was full of lorries and we were constantly in the outside lane, overtaking them. As Hopper talked about buying his book I became aware of the back and side of the driver's head and I realised that under his hat he was bald. It was Handley, the thug that Candy had said Hopper used for his dirty-work. I knew he must be listening to our conversation.

Brignole's, from the outside, was the same as any other large, modern industrial unit on the outskirts of a city. With its painted block walls and great metal roof it could have been a superstore selling carpets or paint. It was only when you drew up to the incongruous classical entrance that it appeared to be anything different. Wide, glazed doors were flanked by Ionic columns, and inside, the small foyer was plushly carpeted and warmly decorated. It was busy with people registering for the auction and inspecting choice items for future sales displayed in glass cabinets.

"Perhaps you could deal with the formalities?" Hopper asked.

"You'll have to do that yourself. I don't mind bidding for you."

"I'll pay you back immediately," he said. "With ten percent extra for your trouble."

"I could use my credit card, I suppose."

"It'll only be a few hundred euro . . . "

"I'm not sure if it's legal for one person to bid and another to pay."

"It's just a box of books."

The woman behind the desk took my details and issued me with a numbered card. She solemnly pointed towards the large, echoing space beyond the foyer.

Inside the main hall, to one side, were row upon row of assembled lots.

"What's the number?" asked Hopper.

"Lot 1052," I said. "I'll help you find it."

"There's no need." He was trying to act casually, but he was too tense. "Go and wait."

At the far end of the hall was a rostrum faced by a hundred or so chairs, very few of which were occupied. I chose one that allowed me to watch Hopper as he walked down through the rows of lots, picking up items at random, with no apparent interest in anything specific. When he found the box of books he sought, he took out a couple and hardly glanced at them, and then a few more. I guessed that my father would have buried *The Dark Return of Time* at the very bottom. Hopper's body-language was anxious, determined, as he excavated the volumes. When he found the book he was after he opened it and flicked through it, now oblivious to everything and everyone around him. Even from a distance I could see a range of expressions pass across his face as he started to read.

There was not much time left before the buyers would be asked to leave that part of the hall, and it was busy. For some reason my eye was drawn to the movement of one person by the furthest of the lots; a woman with dark hair and a long black coat.

Candy had seen Hopper, but he was too engrossed in the book he had come for. When he re-buried it amongst the others, he was left wearing a deep frown and was not looking at anyone else around him.

I didn't need to ask him whether it was the right book when he walked over to me. His affected insouciance was even more unconvincing than before.

"There's a small café," I told him. "We've time for a drink or something to eat."

From his waistcoat pocket he brought out the watch on its chain and shook his head. "We've only got fifteen minutes before the sale starts. Please go down to the front. We don't want to miss it."

"It might still be an hour and a half before your lot comes up."

"I'd rather you went down to the front," he said, trying not to make it sound like an order. If I had been worried by Hopper before, I was really quite frightened of him now that he had so obviously lost his composure. It was prudent to completely ignore the fact that I had seen Candy there, although I sensed that her presence might mean trouble.

"How much would you like me to bid up to?" I asked.

"As much as it takes."

"But what if it goes up to something silly? My credit card limit . . ."

"Just concentrate on getting it, at all costs. I can sort the money out afterwards."

I didn't want to antagonise him, and so I agreed and sat exactly where he had specified. I was worried how much I would have to pay, but consoled myself with the fact that the higher the price, the more I would earn as my commission.

A quarter of an hour later the auction started with the sale of a group of three eighteenth-century watercolours. Several of the early lots were of some interest, but my mind soon wandered, ranging far and wide. I came close to nodding off a couple of times, but the lot that I was interested in was slowly approaching. After an interminable number of porcelain items were sold, the first lot of books was offered and I was able to take an interest. By the time our "*boîte de fiction révélatrice*" was announced I was awake and ready.

I had recently attended several auctions with my father, and I felt quite calm bidding on Hopper's behalf. The auctioneer suggested opening at five hundred euro. I sat still. He quickly suggested four hundred, then two, and when he wearily asked for one hundred I lifted my card. I was slightly annoyed that he accepted the first bid from elsewhere, but he took two hundred from me, and then three from somewhere off to the side of the hall. I bid four and then quickly had to bid six. Before I knew it we were up to a thousand euro.

The auctioneer seemed as surprised as I was, and he took the bidding up slowly, in small amounts, certain it would close at any time. I had resigned myself to insisting that Hopper would have to pay with his own credit card. When the price reached two thousand I was seriously concerned, but I also started to realise that something odd was happening. Then I guessed what the cause might be.

Slowly and inevitably the price rose.

At three thousand euro the auctioneer commented that there must be a rarity in the lot that he hadn't noticed. He asked if there was a gold bar at the bottom of the box and drew a laugh from his audience. He tried asking for three thousand five hundred and got it. I agreed to four thousand and then he immediately managed to get five from elsewhere. I resisted the temptation to see who I was bidding against. There was silence as I bid five thousand five hundred, but then I heard footsteps hurrying down the aisle and I guessed it was Hopper.

The auctioneer asked if I wanted to bid six thousand five hundred euro. Hopper was alongside me, though, angry, and shook his head vehemently.

The lot was sold to "the woman by the window", who was asked to display the number on her card. Standing up, I looked over and saw Candy was unable to do so because she hadn't registered. She was in no position to pay the ludicrous sum she had bid the lot up to.

Hopper was striding away, out of the room, and the auctioneer asked what was going on. Candy was simply staring down at the ground, refusing to communicate, and when he looked at me I was only able to shrug. The auctioneer suggested that all parties should go to the director's office, and that the lot should be considered unsold.

As I walked out I could see that Candy was not moving, and she would not look up. I wanted to go over to her, but even though the auctioneer was trying to sell the next lot, everybody was staring at either her or me.

"Who the hell is meant to be in charge?" Hopper was demanding at the front desk.

A smartly-dressed woman told an usher to fetch Candy out of the hall.

"He was bidding for you?" she asked Hopper, looking at me. "You will all come into my office. The director will be here *immédiatement*."

Hopper, though, told me to stay outside. Through the closed door I could hear voices, although they weren't raised. Some moments later a man in an expensive suit passed me and went in, and then an usher, who left again, almost immediately, with the woman. I still hadn't seen Candy leave the hall.

While I waited, Handley came in through the main entrance. He seemed to have sensed that something was wrong and looked around suspiciously.

"Successful?" he asked me.

"There've been complications."

I was wondering whether I should give him any details, when the office door opened again and Hopper appeared.

"Would you come inside," he invited, obviously suppressing his anger.

"Can I help?" asked Handley.

Hopper shook his head.

In the office the director asked me, "You were bidding on behalf of this gentleman?"

"Yes, for Mr. Hopper."

The door opened and the auctioneer now entered. The director asked me, "Do you know the woman who was bidding against you?"

I glanced at Hopper who gave the slightest shake of his head.

"No," I said dutifully.

"Never seen her before," affirmed Hopper.

"Well, she's just run off," said the auctioneer. "An usher had restrained her but she bit him and escaped. I ought to call the police."

"I don't care about her," said Hopper reasonably. "But I do care about that lot."

"We will have to put it into next month's auction."

"I would like to make the seller an offer for it now."

"But we can't say how much it would have raised? There might have been another potential bidder who was put off by that woman."

"I'm sure we can come to an arrangement that means Brignole's receives its share."

The auctioneer addressed me directly: "What was the maximum you were told to bid up to?"

Without hesitation I said, "A thousand euro."

He raised his eyebrows, looked at the auctioneer and told him to leave. When we were alone the director looked at Hopper, then back at me: "If you are willing to pay one thousand euro I will put it through as a sale, no questions asked."

"Hmm," said Hopper. "Perhaps the woman was working for you? Your guide price was three to four hundred euro."

I wondered why Hopper was quibbling.

"Eight hundred," suggested the auctioneer. "Otherwise you will have to wait until next month's sale."

Hopper agreed and I passed over my credit card. It would probably result in my account becoming overdrawn, but the commission from Hopper would make amends. The man left the room with my card, regarding it suspiciously as though he thought it might be a fake.

"Why did you say a thousand?" asked Hopper. "For that box of old rubbish! You should've said five hundred."

"It has to be worth his while."

"Maybe I do need Handley's help. Wait here."

I did as I was told, though I feared for Candy. I hoped that she would have had the good sense to leave. The auctioneer returned and the money was debited from my card. I was handed a receipt and was told that I could collect the books. I obediently followed him back out into the reception area and was given a heavy box without a lid. He opened the door for me and seemed pleased when I left.

I'd never seen such an unpromising lot. The books gave every impression that they had been stored outside for several months; most of them were misshapen with damp. As I carried them to where Hopper and Handley stood in conversation by the car I peered amongst those I could see on the top. There was nothing that looked as if it might be Hopper's precious volume.

They stopped talking as I approached. The car boot was opened and I put the box inside. Hopper bent over it with some distaste and pulled away those books he did not want. The volume he sought was tatty, a rusty-brown colour, and when he opened it the pages appeared stained.

"Would you like to ride in the front?" he asked me, unimpressed. "You'll see the countryside better on the way back to Paris."

Whatever might have been wrong with my father earlier in the day, he no longer showed any sign of illness.

"Had you told her about the book?" he asked me.

"No!"

"Did she explain why she was bidding for it?"

"Nobody got a chance to talk to her; she ran off."

"Well, if she didn't get the information from me or you, it must've come from Hopper himself. Do you think he might have told her to go to Saint-Quentin so that he could continue the games he's been playing?"

"It's possible."

"More importantly, was he happy with the book?"

"I've no idea. I travelled back in the front of the car and he sat behind me, reading it, saying nothing."

"Did he reimburse you?"

"No; I was just pleased to get out of the car. His chauffeur was Handley; the man Candy said did his dirty work for him."

The phone rang and my father walked back into the office saying, "If you can believe anything she says."

Looking out of the shop window, I wished there was more to stare at than the dusty black van parked outside.

It all but completely obscured the houses opposite. What with the display of books in the window, I couldn't get close enough to the glass to even see the sky.

I heard my father put the phone down. He was grimacing:

"That was Hopper. He's got back home and realised that he drove away with the rest of the books. He asked if I'd like them dropped off here. I said we'd bring them back after we've had dinner with him tonight."

"I really don't want to go."

"I imagine he'll have a cheque waiting for you."

"You can collect it for me."

"We have to go, especially after what happened."

"Did he say anything else?"

"No, not about his book, or that silly girl."

VII.

My father and I were among a dozen guests at Hopper's house. In the elegantly appointed drawing-room we were served champagne, and voices were low in deference to the woman playing the *Gnossiennes* of Satie on the piano in the corner.

Hopper greeted us warmly; he was enjoying playing the generous and genial host. He introduced us to a junior minister from the French Department of Education and suggested, knowingly, that we would have a great deal in common. The man was eager to talk with us in English, but soon found himself forced to discuss, pointlessly, the current French curriculum compared to that which my father had been taught at Grammar School in England thirty years before. The junior minister was unfailingly polite and feigned great interest, and I entertained myself by looking at the modern artwork around the walls, trying to decide whether it was interesting or just pretentious. It should have contrasted with the furniture, which attempted to look antique, but failed to do so because each item was an expensive, modern reproduction.

A second glass of champagne convinced me to try to find the evening amusing. A man in an immaculate artist's smock introduced himself to me as the artist responsible for some of the paintings on the walls, and I asked him a number of deliberately philistine questions, which he answered with good humour. I was certain that Hopper had surrounded himself with people whom he thought would be impressed by the company he kept.

When the time came, it was in a relaxed mood that I made my way with the others down towards the dining room. As I passed the library, however, Hopper contrived, very discreetly, to make me step inside.

With the door not quite closed behind us, he said with the blandest of expressions, "I'll only ask this once, and then the subject need not arise again. Did you tell Candy Smith that we were going to Saint-Quentin to bid on my book?"

"No."

"Then the subject is closed," he smiled and handed me a cheque. "I rounded-up your commission," he said.

I was sure that he didn't believe me. Why should he? Standing in close proximity to the man, alone, I knew that I shouldn't make an enemy of him.

My concerns were soon forgotten, though. When I sat down at the large table I quickly drank the wine served with the first course, and very soon I was talking to the young woman on my left. Hortense had recently begun a "doctorat" in English Literature and was really very pretty. We were soon arguing, good-naturedly, the merits of certain authors. My father had also found himself next to a congenial neighbour and was discussing shop rents in Paris.

Because the party was quite a large one, inevitably there were several simultaneous conversations. On a number of occasions, though, Hopper insisted on breaking off discussion at his end of the table and asking the opinion of me or my father on literary matters. Hopper had been discussing with the junior minister which books should be read in French schools. He asked me and my father whether any country was able to recognise its own classics, and whether the opinion of foreigners had any relevance. The junior minister professed a belief that literary work could only be properly appreciated if read in the language it was written.

Hortense agreed: "Otherwise you are at the mercy of translators!"

"But when a book is recognised as being of international significance . . . ?" my father asked.

"The English can never understand French authors!" announced a woman to whom I had not been introduced. "Balzac, Dumas, Flaubert, Zola, Proust, Camus . . . "

"By your logic, the French can never fully understand English writers," my father countered, and began a list of his own: "Shakespeare, Byron, Keats, Shelley, Dickens . . ."

"The English refuse to read intellectual authors!" the woman countered. She had too many small teeth, and refused to make any further contribution.

The argument was spirited. Hortense brought up Houellebecq and the table was split over his importance. Talk veered off in different directions and fragmented, but several times during the meal Hopper attempted to get the whole table involved in the discussion of literature.

Over dessert I suddenly realised that Hopper was drunk, and not able to disguise the fact. Although the various conversations around the table had moved on, Hopper declared with gravity and too-careful enunciation: "I've not discovered anything else, apart from books, that allows us to explore the complexities of human experience and emotions. Film, music, poetry; they all have their place, but they're too limited."

Out of respect for our host we had all gone quiet. It was my father who carefully agreed with Hopper and moved the talk forward once more.

When the dinner party was over and we were walking back past the library Hopper caught my eye and inclined his head towards the door. I warily followed him inside once more, afraid that he would want to talk about Candy Smith again.

Slightly slurring his words he said, "Flavian, please understand that I trust you." Although he was holding himself together, he reminded me of a drunk who had decided to emotionally declare his love for a fellow-drinker.

"Thank you," I said primly, quite affected by the alcohol myself, but on my guard.

He nodded to the box of books that I recognised from that afternoon, "They're yours. I hope you can make some money out of them. Personally, I wouldn't give any of them house-room; not in that state."

I didn't want to ask him, but it seemed right to enquire, "I hope that copy of *The Dark Return of Time* was worth all the trouble?"

"I don't quite know what to make of it."

"It *is* in very poor condition."

"That's not really the reason."

"Perhaps the problem is the attainment of the quest?"

"I don't understand."

"When you've been hunting for anything for a long time, it can sometimes be a let-down when you find it. If the search for your Holy Grail is over, what else is there to do with your time?"

"No, that's not it. It's the subject matter."

"Is it about you?" I asked.

He looked directly at me. "It concerns all of us," he said, slightly sententiously. "But I'm also wondering how many other copies there might be out there, and whether it's possible to track them all down."

"It's obviously rare. But that copy turned up soon enough after we started searching."

"That was pre-ordained."

"In what way?"

He shook his head, and then nodded towards the box of books:

"Pick them up another time," he said. He put his arm around me, and together we walked back to the drawing room.

We left not long afterwards. My father was feeling mellow after all of the food and wine, and wanted to discuss his neighbour at the table.

"Ernestine has a position of some influence in the Parisian *Chambre de commerce*," he was saying. "And she's a very cultured woman."

I let him talk on, but cut him short when he asked me what I thought of Hortense.

"But you two seemed to be getting on so well," he said with a knowing wink.

The night air was cold and had sobered me up a little; "I'm suspicious. Do you think Hopper carefully selected Ernestine and Hortense for you and me."

"If he did then all it shows is that he's a considerate host."

"But do you think he paid them to be there?"

"As up-market escorts? If he did then he thinks more of us than I thought!"

"I don't know. It was all too good to be true."

"Why question everything so deeply? Perhaps we really should take the man at face value. He's got money and likes to share it. There's every chance that those two women are having the same conversation concerning us."

"I doubt it! What have we got to offer? You in your little bookshop and me not knowing what I'm meant to be doing with my life."

We were in the rue Berthe by that time and my father stopped suddenly: "Go home and get some sleep, Flavian. Hopefully you won't be so maudlin in the morning."

I wondered if Paris, or any other city, ever really got dark, or truly quiet. I would have liked it to have done so that evening. The restaurants and bars were closing for the night and there were few people abroad, but even when I passed a street that was apparently empty, there were lights burning in windows above the shops, and I was constantly aware of distant voices or cars. I was annoyed by its indifference towards me, and dwelt on my feelings of resentment. It meant that, for the first time since it happened, I passed through the Passage des Abbesses without thinking about the abduction. I was aimlessly walking down towards the Metro, trying to imagine all the voids beneath my feet full of moving underground trains, of water, electricity cables and sewerage. My thoughts were rather muddled; I was not admitting to myself where I was going, or why. However, I was forced to confront exactly where I was when I turned into the rue des Martyrs. There were flashing blue lights coming from the rue André Gill, reflecting off all the windows in the vicinity. The air reeked, harsh and acrid, of smoke. I had detected it from quite a distance away without any idea of its import.

A number of vehicles, including a fire engine, blocked the rue des Martyrs and there were hoses laid out down the street. There were more fire engines and hoses in the cul-de-sac itself. People in uniform pushed past in the artificial and flashing lights, and the ground was gritty and wet beneath my shoes.

I managed to get quite close to Candy's building before a fireman stopped me. He patiently listened to my questions and assumed that, as I was a foreigner, I wanted access to the hotel.

"*Il a été evacuée,*" he explained, taking me by the arm to the opposite pavement. As he did so I looked up in vain for a sight of Candy's windows; all I could see was darkness and I knew it was terribly wrong. The streetlamps gave no clues; they simply deepened the shadows on the top floors. The first floor windows were also black, the glass had disappeared, but at least I could see that part of the building was still standing.

I asked what had happened.

"*Un grand feu, monsieur.*"

"Was anyone hurt?"

"*Je ne sais pas,*" he said, and then carefully, in English. "A young woman lived there. *Elle ne peut pas avoir survécu!*"

I thought I understood; "She can't have survived?"

"*Je ne sais pas,*" he repeated. "*Les investigateurs retourneront le matin.*" He shook his head and repeated: "*C'était un grand feu.*"

My father was not answering the telephones in either his apartment or the shop, and though he was proud of his mobile phone, he rarely turned it on. I imagined the conversation I would have been having with him if he had actually answered any of them. I would have said that Candy's building had been burnt down by Hopper in revenge for what she had done at the auction, and he would have asked what proof I had. He'd have asked why Hopper would bother going to such lengths when he was able to keep Candy distant by playing the games he did. In turn, I'd have said that it was all too much of a coincidence, and my father would've pointed out, quite rightly, that she was a drunk, convicted of attempted murder, living in Paris illegally. Wasn't it more likely that she'd burnt the place down herself? The imaginary debate went round and around in my head and I could only stifle it by drinking more wine.

I overslept the following morning and phoned the shop to tell my father I would be in late. Despite the long discussion I had rehearsed the night before, I now simply told him that there had been a fire, and that I didn't know if Candy was alive or dead.

"The poor girl," was his reply, and there seemed nothing else to say.

My head hurt and I felt dizzy. I took aspirins, drank glasses of water, shaved and showered. Then I downed a succession of cups of coffee, using them as an excuse for not leaving the haven of my apartment.

When I eventually went out, I found a café on the rue des Abbesses where I was able to order a large and greasy breakfast, and yet more coffee. It fortified me sufficiently to be able to go back to the rue André Gill. I don't know quite what I expected to find there. My head had stopped hurting by that time, but I still felt tired. The street was a mess, but two men with brushes and a hose were attempting to clear up the debris. Workmen were boarding up the doors and lower windows of Candy's building.

It looked as though the fire had raged vertically. When I looked up, it was not simply that the roof had been burnt out; the whole top floor was missing. Whether or not I was miscounting the storeys, the complete destruction of Candy's rooms was clear.

A young policeman came out from the hotel entrance and took out a notebook and pen. When I asked him about the fire he shook his head and there were tears in his eyes: "*Nous supposons qu'elle est morte*," he said. He stared down at his notebook and started to write, steadfastly refusing to say any more.

It was midday when I made it into the bookshop. By that time I had decided that my father's imagined comments from the night before were what I wanted to believe.

"Any news?" he asked, and I said "no". I was pleased that he, too was disinclined to talk, and I wondered if he had indulged in the same fictional conversation.

"I hate to bring this up," he said, producing a book from under the counter. It was *The Horse's Mouth*, by Joyce Cary. "What shall we do with it"

"I'll take it round to him. The thought of it lying there all day, while I try and work, is too much."

"I'm not sure if you should; not right now."

For once Hopper's door was not answered promptly. I had to press the button on the intercom for a second time before I was brusquely asked my business in bad French.

"I've a book for Mr. Hopper."

"He's in a meeting," said a voice with an unmistakable London accent. "Come back later."

I had been trying to suppress my confused anger, but the disembodied order was an opportunity to release it.

"It's a book your boss asked for especially," I insisted. "He won't appreciate it if you turn me away."

There was another delay, but the door opened. A large man towered over me and put out an over-sized hand.

"I'll take it for him," he said.

"How long will his meeting last? I can wait."

"I'll give it to him."

"You don't understand the importance of this book?" I pushed my luck. "I'd like to take it through to the library. I'm Mr. Hopper's new librarian."

The doorman was as annoyed by me as I was by him. He stood to one side and let me past, but then followed me, closely, all the way to the door of the library. I could hear raised voices from further along the corridor.

Once inside the room, I put the book down on the desk and turned to address the man who had shown me in.

"A cup of tea would be nice," I said, "while I'm waiting."

"I don't make tea."

"So go and find somebody who does . . . "

I was surprised at myself, but derived a great deal of satisfaction from ordering the thug around.

Alone, I was at a loss to know what to do, so I took out my glasses and looked over the shelves. I had yet to do any work as Hopper's librarian, and I wasn't sure that I ever would. Despite my anger, the bibliophile in me couldn't help but notice that a very few of the man's Octavo Society volumes had dustjackets. If there had been more, I might have wasted several lucrative hours slipping them inside protective plastic sleeves. The books were arranged alphabetically by author and I supposed that I could have created fiction and non-fiction sections, although it wouldn't have taken somebody with a degree to do that. Compiling a catalogue might have been worthwhile; I could have justified that because it would act as an inventory for insurance purposes. Not that many of them had any real value.

As I disdainfully regarded Hopper's shelves it struck me that it might be worth trying to read a little of *The Dark Return of Time*. As I didn't know who had written it I wasn't sure where it would be, but I remembered the rusty brown cloth. To my annoyance there was nothing of that description at either end of the alphabetised books, or on a small shelf of miscellaneous volumes behind the desk.

I took off my glasses and went to the door. Down the corridor the volume of the voices rose and fell from time to time, but even at their loudest I couldn't make out what was being said. Curiosity tempted me down the corridor, where I pretended to inspect the dull, modern pictures on the walls, idly wondering if they were originals or prints. Unfortunately, as I passed a door, it opened.

"What the fuck are you doing?" Handley demanded, grabbing my arm.

I gasped and dropped my spectacles. It took a second before I could exhale and reply. My heart was beating in double time and I knew that I must have looked guilty.

The man asked again, his voice lower but the threat of violence increased. I managed to say, "I'm here about Mr. Hopper's library."

His hold on my arm remained tight, painful even, and he turned me around and marched me towards the room from which I'd come. I said I'd dropped my glasses, but he ignored me. I hadn't realised before what a tall man he was; he held me high so that I could barely touch the carpet. My anger and petulance had turned to fear and I wasn't going to attempt to argue.

As we reached the library door the first man arrived with a tray bearing my tea. The two exchanged confused glances and within a few seconds I was in the room, alone. This time I was able to eavesdrop on the discussion. Handley was demanding an explanation.

I started to tremble just as I had done when I'd witnessed the abduction in the Passage des Abbesses. The way that I had been taken hold of reminded me of the way that the men in the balaclavas had held the naked couple. It had been a powerful enough grip, but I knew that there was much more strength there if required. Handley had done his job with an assurance similar to that of the men in the Passage. In comparing the height of both of Hopper's men, with their broad shoulders and muscular build, with those I'd seen at the abduction, they were too similar for it to be a coincidence. I felt a sudden need to sit down.

I had been a fool, creeping down the hallway towards the mysterious voices like some character from an Enid Blyton adventure. I had been so sure of myself, not only because of a naïve sense of right and wrong, but due to a stupid belief in my own invulnerability. But now I was sure that the men in the house were also those from the Passage, it would imply that Candy had been telling the truth; Hopper *had* been behind the abduction, torture and deaths. And if he had burnt down Candy's building, probably with her inside, what might he do to me?

I waited with a sense of mounting dread. I had to sit down, but my shaking would not stop. I decided that if Hopper did not arrive within five minutes I would get up and try to leave. I took deep breaths, trying to keep calm. I thought through my exit and rehearsed the words I would use if challenged by his men. Perhaps, I considered, it might be a good time to return to England. Suddenly the idea of being safe, even living with my mother, was very tempting.

The second hand on my watch moved slowly, and the minute hand apparently not at all. Before my self-imposed time limit was up, there were footsteps in the hallway. The door opened and Hopper entered, alone. He appeared to be calm.

"What did you overhear?" he asked.

"Nothing," I replied. I knew how defensive I sounded, and how tremulous my voice was. "I was just waiting for you, looking at the pictures in the corridor, when one of your thugs grabbed me and frog-marched me back in here."

"I apologise. He knew you were here about the books and thought it odd that you were wandering around the house."

I couldn't answer that, and didn't try to. Instead, I pointed to the small parcel on his desk: "I brought you the first edition of *The Horse's Mouth.*"

"Thank you," he smiled, slightly absently. "You can take away the Octavo Society copy now."

He handed me my glasses and picked up the parcel from the desk. He couldn't resist opening it.

"You referred to Handley and Franklin as my 'thugs'," he said, taking the book out and putting it on the arm of his chair after only a cursory glance. "The description's not inappropriate. But what worries me is the way your mind seems to be working at the moment."

"Oh?" I tried to affect calmness.

"From here I can almost see the cogs whirring in your brain, the tumblers moving into place. And I know exactly who's set your thoughts in this odd direction. I do understand your suspicions.'

I couldn't stop myself from saying, "Candy was sure you set up the abduction."

"In the Passage des Abbesses? Yes, that's *exactly* how her mind works, sadly."

"She told me you were involved. And now her apartment's been burnt out, with her in it."

An expression of annoyance crossed his face, at which point fear gripped my chest. He considered his reply for a few seconds.

"There's been a fire at Candy's apartment?"

"It was gutted."

"And they've found her body?"

"No, well, we assume it'll be in there."

"*Who's* assuming that?"

"The firemen, the police . . . "

He shook his head gravely: "I'd like to think you're wrong. I'll do what I can to find out. But do you really believe I arranged for her to be killed?"

"I don't know what to think."

He shook his head again.

"I know that you don't like the relationship I have with Candy. Neither do I. Don't you think I could have simply told the authorities where to find her? Then she'd have been sent back to England.

"I'm involved in many businesses, Flavian. I like making contacts with people who can help me. I suppose I can be pretty ruthless, and it sounds a little dramatic, but there *are* people out there who I should probably call enemies. And it's unfortunate that I have to employ men like Handley and Franklin, but they're good for fetching and carrying. Yes, they can put the frighteners on people, if need be, but there is another side to me. It's the side that likes music and books. I love art and appreciate fine wine and women. I'm sentimental about them all! I promise you that if Candy Smith is dead I'll be seriously upset."

He took up his telephone and pressed a single number.

"Handley, there's been a fire at the apartment of my old friend Candy Smith. Look into it will you, discreetly, and make sure she's okay. Thank you."

He put the phone down. "I understand you're worried, but don't think the worst until we know for sure. My man has a few contacts, we'll have the information soon enough."

I stood up, hoping to leave, but not daring to think I would be allowed to.

"I don't want you to believe that I'm the man Candy claims," he seemed to be genuinely saddened. "My main weakness is a lack of culture and education. Really, I'd prefer not to have any business concerns; I'd rather retire and read and discuss books. My dream is to end my days in the great museums and libraries of the capital cities of Europe."

"So why not sell your businesses and retire?"

"It's not that easy. You can't just shut yourself off from the world you've created. People won't let you, and anyway, I need educated men like you and your father to help me. I need your advice to amass a fine library. A Monsieur Grillet is advising me on art," he said, and smiled. "And you will help me sweep away all these Octavo Society books!"

I laughed, despite myself. Hopper opened the door and as we walked out he asked, "What was the first Sherlock Holmes book?"

"*A Study in Scarlet.*"

"And how much will a copy set me back?"

"A nice copy of the first edition, first issue, would be, perhaps, seventy-five thousand euro."

"A first issue?"

It was ludicrous to be discussing the niceties of book collecting, but it was a relief. It was so unlikely, so stupidly melodramatic, that the man before me could ever have had me taken away and tortured by Franklin and Handley. I explained:

"There was meant to be a mistake in the first few copies printed that wasn't in later ones."

"So it'll cost me more to have a copy with a mistake in it? I'll have to think about that."

I was wrong about the first issue of *A Study in Scarlet*; oddly enough the later issue contains the mistake, not the first. The details came up as an aside in a long and circuitous discussion with my father. As we talked, all my suspicion of Hopper returned.

"If he orders a copy of *A Study in Scarlet* then it's obvious that he's paying us off," I insisted. "Candy seriously upset him and now she's dead."

"It may be a coincidence, and we don't know for sure she is . . ."

"So you just want to go along with all this? You want to make what you can out of Hopper?"

"I don't want any money from him if he's a crook . . ."

"He's not just a crook. He's a murderer!"

" . . . And I don't want to take any risks."

"So what are you going to do?"

"If I go and see him . . . "

"You mustn't."

"What I was going to say was that *if* I go and see him, I'm not sure I'll come away any the wiser. I'll still be suspicious. And I certainly don't want to annoy him."

"So what do we do?"

"I think that *you* have to go to the police with your suspicions."

"So far they've taken very little interest in anything I have had to say."

"But at least your conscience would be clear."

VIII.

The interview room was narrow, sterile and knowing. The policeman who entered glanced down at a sheet of paper, bored, and said, "Monsieur Bennett . . . " He then remembered, amusement animating his features: "Flavian!"

We'd previously met in the Passage des Abbesses.

"I'm worried about Candy Smith. There was a fire last night where she lived in the rue André Gill."

"I have been told about the fire. But it is still too soon to understand what happened. Do you have some information?"

"She was employed by Reginald Hopper. She recently upset him by bidding on a book at auction that he wanted. She tried to spoil the sale . . . "

"May I record this conversation? Otherwise I will have to take down notes, and switch between English, and writing in French . . . "

I agreed, but while he found a cassette and put it in the machine, my composure withered. Once the little wheels were going around, I found it hard to make the direct accusations that I had planned. I relied heavily on reporting what Candy had told me, having explained who she was and why she was in Paris. The policeman let me ramble on, asking questions from time to time, and I could hear how circumstantial and unlikely it all sounded. The policeman was polite throughout, and when I finished, he switched off the tape recorder.

"I will talk to Monsieur Hopper," he promised. "And to Monsieurs Handley and Franklin. I need to find more information regarding Mademoiselle Smith, but your suspicions will be thoroughly investigated. Now, I have your address . . . "

"Yes, but I'm not sure that I'll be in Paris much longer."

The idea had come to me earlier that day as I'd waited for Hopper in his study, and now that I had actually articulated it, I felt some relief. It struck me as cowardly to leave, but prudent. I would have to discuss the decision with my father, of course. Leaving him behind felt wrong, and my concern for him was the only reason I didn't immediately pack up my belongings when I arrived back at the apartment.

The insistent ringing of the doorbell sounded loud; four floors below somebody wanted me urgently. It was only just becoming light and I ran into the main room, sure that something was wrong. I pressed the button and asked who was calling, worried, for some reason, that it might be Hopper, or my father. It occurred to me that it might even be Candy. However, a voice informed me that it was the police, and I released the lock on the door down below.

When the knock came at the door to the apartment itself I checked at the security squint and could see two uniformed officers. The first man to enter had more buttons and braid on his uniform than the one following him. In the time it had taken them to get up the stairs I had put on a dressing gown, but wearing my pyjamas I felt at a distinct disadvantage.

"What's happened?" I asked.

"*Vous avez parlé à un de mes supérieurs hier au sujet du feu sur les rue des Martyres? Et vous avez posé des questions sur Candy Smith?*"

I must have looked blank, and he repeated the question in English. "You asked about the fire. You asked about

Candy Smith?" He chose his words carefully: "I must tell you, there has been an *enquête préliminaire* . . . "

"A preliminary investigation?

"*Oui*. The report is not official, but it is believed that the fire was started *délibérément*."

"Deliberately?"

"*Sur the rez-de-chaussée*, the ground floor, *dans la cage d'escalier* . . . " He looked at me and then his colleague, but unaided he translated this as "in the stairwell".

With inappropriate satisfaction he said, with a sudden upward movement of his hands: "The building went—whoosh! The door to the top was open. That is why it was *complètement brûlé*. The other apartments are damaged; smoke, water . . . *Les investigateurs* examined every floor but report no bodies. They have not found Candy Smith."

I was relieved, and finally asked them to sit down, which they did, although they gave the impression that they would rather be somewhere else.

"But why are you here at six in the morning?" I asked.

"I am working, *monsieur*. And my superior told me, I must tell you, that there is no body of Candy Smith."

"But you are still searching for her?"

"Of course! First, we ask the landlord. He is foreign, Spanish, and believed the building to be *vide*, empty. He lets the building fall down because he wants permission to *reconstruisez*, ah, construct a new building, but the *planificateurs de ville*, they say no. So, we do not have information that anybody lived in the top apartment."

"But I told your superior, I went inside, and Candy Smith was definitely living there. It was run down . . . "

"She was not there officially, but yes, somebody had been living there."

"Have you talked to Reginald Hopper? He admitted to me that he was paying her. He may have organised her accommodation as well."

"*Oui*, we have talked to Monsieur Hopper. He asks, why would he burn her accommodation when he could just report to the police that she was in France illegally?"

"Because he was angry with her! You investigated what happened at the auction."

"We have discussed this with colleagues in Saint-Quentin and there was a woman there. She placed a bid but did not pay. The auctioneer was wrong to sell you the books."

"That's not important. What happened to Candy is important. If she wasn't in the fire, where is she now?"

"We do not know. We have consulted the police in Britain and she is wanted by them. She had disappeared. We had not been searching for her before, but we will be now."

"I'm very worried about her."

"Was she a friend? Or was she just somebody who told you her . . . her suspicions of Mr. Hopper?"

"Just a friend."

"Our investigations show that Monsieur Hopper is a businessman, and he has a strange past. But, *il n'est pas venu à notre attention*. We are not interested in him."

"He employs a man called Handley, and another called Franklin. I don't trust either of them."

"We take seriously what you have reported to us. I promise that we will talk to everyone."

"But, tell me, those poor people who were taken from the Passage des Abbesses?"

"That investigation continues," he said, in a tone that suggested that no more information would be forthcoming. "Another colleague deals with that."

"But if it's related to Hopper, like the fire, and Candy . . . ?"

"*Rapportée?* We do not believe it. They are different cases."

He stood up, followed by the other officer, and thanked me for my time. The second then mumbled something to the first, who turned to me:

"If you see Candy Smith, please tell us. We must speak to her."

They left, and as I was up and awake, I washed and dressed. When I had finished breakfast it was too early to go to the shop and once again I considered packing my few belongings. I couldn't quite make the decision.

Bennett's British Bookshop doesn't normally open until ten, but that morning it did so at half past eight, to the annoyance of my father who came down to investigate. An hour later I had re-dressed the window, a job we had been putting off for weeks, and when my father came down at his usual time he appeared to be in a better mood. I was starting to tell him about my visit from the police when the clock behind the counter chimed the customary opening hour. Immediately afterwards a vehicle passed very slowly in the street. I recognised it as Hopper's.

I felt sick. I looked through the glass in the door and could see that the car was being parked. At the angle I was watching from I could just see Handley walk around to the back and open the boot. He then removed the box of books that had been bought at the auction. Somebody else closed the boot for him.

I considered changing the sign on the door to "*fermé*", but as my father was behind the counter I decided, instead, to slip into the back. I left the office door only slightly open, and sat down before the computer as though I was doing some work.

From where I was hiding I could hear my father greet the visitors with a more subdued "Good morning" than was usual for him. I heard the box being put down, heavily, on the counter.

"The deal is that they're now yours," Hopper said. "Your commission."

"Thank you, but haven't you paid Flavian already?"

"I have, but I have no need for these."

"Then thank you. I'm not sure that many of them can be offered as anything other than 'reading copies' . . . "

"No, it was my book that appears to've been worth eight hundred euro . . . However, at least I have it now."

Hopper's tone was neutral and I was feeling reassured until he added, "I would like to have a word with Flavian, if I may?"

"He's in the office," said my father, and, inevitably, a moment later Hopper was standing just outside. Although he could see me through the partly open door he still knocked.

"Good morning. I was wondering if we could talk."

I had started to tremble, but said as levelly as I could: "I'm not sure there's anything to discuss."

Hopper came in and closed the door carefully behind him.

"Oh, but there is. You see, I've had the police asking me all kinds of questions. I think they've been talking to you."

"And you're annoyed with me?"

"You went to see them?"

"Yes. I'm concerned about Candy."

"So am I. But she wasn't in the fire. Did they tell you that?"

"They did."

"But she is, nevertheless, missing. This is all very awkward, but I wanted to clear the air. I want you to trust me, but I understand that after everything she has told you that it's not easy. All I'll say is that I understand why you went to the police. All this stems from that day in the Passage des Abbesses, doesn't it?"

I nodded.

He considered, "I should've really stayed and talked to the police. Not that it would've helped."

He came to an awkward halt, then put out his hand:

"Flavian, I assure you that I'm not the monster that Candy believed me to be."

"Believed?"

He frowned.

"Past tense," I explained.

"I'm not as educated as you. I don't want there to be any bad feelings between us."

With him standing over me I found it impossible not to get up and take his hand. His grip was firm and he held my hand just a little too long.

"Good," he said simply. As he left the office he said over his shoulder:

"I hope you'll still come and help me out in my library? I would appreciate your services."

"Of course, anything we can do to help," replied my father.

"I have to admit that visits from the police have put me off Sherlock Holmes," Hopper said. "I need another recommendation; like *Le Grand Meaulnes*, or *The Horse's Mouth*."

"Those are rather different books," replied my father. "But I may have something else for you."

He came through to the office and took down a copy of *The Quest for Corvo* by A.J.A. Symons.

I knew that I ought to follow him out into the shop. I didn't want to appear to be hiding, but I didn't want to be in the same room as Hopper.

"*Literary* detection," I heard my father explain, presumably handing the book to Hopper.

"And will the first edition set me back as much as *A Study in Scarlet*?"

"No, no, this copy is a first, but it's only a couple of hundred euro."

"In that case I have confidence in your judgement and will write you a cheque now. I trust you, Mr. Bennett. I just wish your son would trust *me*."

"Oh, he's all right," said my father airily. "His girlfriend died a little while ago and his mood is, understandably, all over the place. He's upset about Candy because she reminded him of this girl."

I was furious with my father, but incredulous when I heard Hopper quietly reply, "I know".

"But it's none of your business!" I shouted at my father once Hopper and Handley had left. He apologised, which made it hard to have an argument, although I tried my best to prolong it. The remainder of the day dragged interminably; if we had been busy with customers it would have been easier, but there weren't any and the phone did not ring. I spent the morning trying to clean up the books from the auction. Half of them had to be thrown away, but the others were quite respectable when they had been brushed down and their dust jackets put into protective plastic. There were a couple of Ruth Rendell first editions, albeit American ones, that almost passed as new by the time I had finished with them. When each was made as respectable as it could be, my father typed up descriptions, researched the prices, and uploaded them to sites on the internet. By the early afternoon we had finished, but I determinedly stayed until closing time. By the end of the day I regretted that there had been any kind of atmosphere between myself and my father, and I was pleased when he agreed to go to the Ciné 13 theatre on Avenue Junot with me that evening.

By unspoken, mutual consent we did not talk about anything that might start an argument for over a week. I didn't mention to my father that I was thinking of leaving Paris; I tried not to think about it myself.

Part Two

I.

I have never really liked spiders; it's their sudden motion, or the possibility of it, that worries me. The long-legged specimen lurking on the shelf behind the travel guides appeared to be dead, but when I went to brush it away it darted out of sight, causing me to jump back.

I dropped the books I was holding, and felt doubly foolish because two men in suits had entered the shop at that moment. The first did not seem to have noticed my embarrassment; he immediately asked:

"Do you have anything by Ruth Rendell?"

I directed him to the shelf of contemporary crime novels, and then picked up the books I had dropped. The second man had already turned his attention to the paperbacks by the door.

Taking the fallen books to the counter I affected to be inspecting them for any damage, although I was really peering over the top of my spectacles at the first customer. He had found the four titles by Rendell and considered them for a moment before taking down the first American edition of *A Demon in My View*. It was the copy from the sale at Brignole's, and he immediately slipped the jacket off and appraised the maroon lettering on the tan cloth spine. There was a black mark at the bottom that I had been unable to remove and I guessed that this was what he was looking for. I watched him give the man who had come in with him the slightest of nods, and then he re-jacketed the book.

"May I ask where you obtained this?" he asked me. His manner was relaxed.

"At an auction at Saint-Quentin. Why?"

"You are Flavian Bennett?"

He put his hand in his pocket and brought out a small black wallet. He showed me a business card; printed on it was a small symbol of a sword, scales and a globe.

"My name is Saunders. My colleague is Grillet. We work for the International Criminal Police Organisation," he explained.

I must have looked disbelieving.

"Interpol. We investigate crimes that overlap several member countries. In this case, we are making investigations that interest both the French and British police."

My father came out of the office. He had been listening, and said, "Would you like to talk to these gentlemen in my apartment?"

"Thank you," I said, and gestured towards the door that led up the precipitous stairs. "Would you like to follow me?"

My father's rooms were always fussily tidy, despite the number of books that had migrated up there from the shop over the years. The living room had a sofa that I suggested the two men sit on, while I took the armchair on the other side of the coffee table. They looked comical, sitting side by side, but they were in earnest.

"You know Reginald Hopper," the first man stated. "We've read the statements you've given the police. We've been told of your suspicions. We're particularly interested in that lot of books that you bid on for Hopper in Saint-Quentin."

"He only wanted one book from it. He let us have the rest as a part of our commission."

"What particular book did he want?"

"*The Dark Return of Time.*"

The second man produced a notebook and wrote down the title.

"The author?"

"It was anonymous."

"Do you have any idea why he wanted it?"

"No."

"He was willing to pay five thousand euro for it."

"He actually paid a lot less, even when you add on the commission he paid me."

"We understand that you paid the auction house eight hundred euro. That was an irregular transaction, but of no interest to us. What we'd like to know is why he wanted that book?"

"I'm not sure. I get the impression that he thinks it might be about him. Or, at least, relates to him."

The man raised his eyebrows:

"You sell books to Mr. Hopper?"

"Yes. And I'm meant to be helping him with his library."

He turned to his colleague and said quietly and quickly in French, "*Une entrée?*"

"You have access to his books?"

"I suppose so, yes, though not *The Dark Return of Time*. I don't know where he keeps that. It wasn't on his shelves the last time I was there."

"Would you be willing to help us in our investigations?"

"I'm not sure; I get the impression Hopper may be a dangerous man. He said he wasn't too annoyed that I'd gone to the police, but if he knew I was actually helping you . . . "

"It really is the best way of discovering what happened to your friend, Candy."

"She's not really my friend . . . "

"But you are worried about her? Of course you are, and we are too."

"So you've no idea what's happened to her?"

"We're specifically investigating Hopper, but Miss Smith's disappearance, and her previous history with him, are not unrelated."

"And those two people who were abducted, and ended up dead in the Seine?"

The second man said to his colleague, again sotto voce, "*Il ne se produira pas. Il est impliqué.*"

"Mr. Bennett," the first man asked. "We would like a favour from you?"

"If I can help."

"We won't try to persuade you to do anything you don't want to. And we certainly don't want to put you in any danger."

"That sounds fine by me."

"All we ask is that you let us see the next book that you sell Mr. Hopper."

"Why?"

"It's best you're not told the details. But it would help us immeasurably."

"That's all?"

"Yes."

"Well, it's downstairs. We recently sold him a copy of *The Quest for Corvo*, and a couple of days ago he asked for a first edition of Corvo's *Hadrian the Seventh*."

"If we might be allowed to borrow it, it'll be returned to you later this afternoon."

I found it easy not to ask why they wanted the book. I managed to pass it to them while my father was busy with a customer and so he didn't realise it had gone. I was concerned because it was a very nice copy with the illustration stamped crisply in white on the purple cloth. I wondered if the whole thing wasn't an obscure and elaborate hoax to try and steal a book, and I had to hold my nerve. If the men were genuine then the situation was rather surreal. I had felt once before as though I had stumbled into a children's adventure story, and it now appeared to have restarted. I even had to look up Interpol to see if they really existed outside of books written in the 1950s.

A woman came in later that afternoon and left *Hadrian the Seventh* on the counter, in a paper bag. It seemed that our visitors had been genuine. She made the bland comment that it was from Monsieur Saunders, and left as nonchalantly as she had arrived.

I put the book back into the office, but my father saw me and asked what I was doing.

"Best not to ask any questions," I said, hoping that it was enough, but a few minutes later he went back into the office and I knew I should follow him. I found him flicking through the pages of the book.

"They didn't explain why they wanted it," I said.

"I suppose you'd better take it to Hopper. We're going to ask five hundred euro for it."

"Now?"

"Whenever," he said, passing it to me. "I don't understand what you're up to."

"Nor do I."

Franklin answered the door and looked down at me disdainfully. He showed me through to the library, where Hopper got up from his desk and seemed genuinely pleased to see me. He took the parcel with some delight.

"So, this is *Hadrian the Seventh*. But is it any good?" he asked.

"I only got half way through it myself. That was a few years ago, though. It starts well, but goes off-the-boil. Corvo was a strange man."

"So I gather."

Hopper appraised the boards. It was a good copy, despite its age, and he opened it up and scanned through a few pages appreciatively. I tried not to think about Saunders's interest in it.

"I *will* read this," he said, as though he thought that I doubted him. "And I might even start collecting Corvo."

"I'm not sure he's really worth collecting. He didn't write the kind of books that many people would want."

"You don't believe in collecting just for the sake of it?"

"No. Books are primarily to be read. But people want books for a myriad of different reasons, I suppose."

"They do," he said slowly, and with such a lack of expression that I was suspicious.

I was sure that it *wasn't* meant to be a cue to ask after *The Dark Return of Time*, but I saw it as a challenge.

"Did you read the book you bought at Brignole's?" I asked.

"Yes."

"And is it about you?"

"It appears to be about somebody I might have been, once, in a previous life."

"Have you any idea who wrote it?"

"No. There're no clues at all."

He walked over to a big heavy, old safe that sat on the floor beside his desk. It could have been Victorian, and when he knelt down, the key he used to unlock it was elaborate and old-fashioned.

From where I stood I could see that the safe was full of bank notes and papers, and on the top shelf was the copy of *The Dark Return of Time*. When he took it out and put it on the desk in front of me it seemed to be in an even poorer condition than I remembered. It had been affected by damp and the boards wouldn't have been able to lie true to the pages inside even if they hadn't also been misshapen. When I lifted the front cover I could see the dark brown staining to the pages which were dirty, creased and torn, and barely clinging to the broken spine. I certainly wouldn't have wanted to own it; muck was coming off it onto my hands.

"The book's beyond any repair," I said. "Even rebinding it wouldn't help."

"It has no value as a physical object. Open it at random and see what you think."

I put on my glasses and unwillingly opened the book at an arbitrary point. I read:

> When the young man in spectacles left the book behind in the house it was in the belief that he was helping to find the missing girl. However, it was not her that he really wanted to help as much as it was the dead woman she reminded him of. He may have blamed his mother for the accident, but *he* had been the one to insist that he could not drive her to work that morning . . .

I jumped, as if the words on the page had suddenly moved, like the spider in the shop that morning.

II.

I left Hopper's house desperately trying to hide my agitation. I didn't analyse what I had read; I simply told myself that I really had to leave Paris, and as soon as possible. My father listened to my reasons, but refused to consider leaving the city himself. I pleaded with him, but he was adamant that he would stay. I explained several times why I thought Hopper and his people were dangerous. I pointed out how suspicious Candy's disappearance was. The only thing I didn't mention was what I had read in his book.

I tried calling my mother, but back in Edgeware she was not answering the phone. I made sure, though, that I booked my ticket that afternoon, for a flight next morning; I was afraid of staying in Paris out of inertia.

My father dutifully called the owner of my apartment to say that I was leaving. Although I insisted that a neighbour could be persuaded to look after the fish, the owner decided that he would come back later the next day to make those arrangements for himself.

I felt less panicked once my return was announced, my seat on the aeroplane booked, and now I only had accommodation for one last night. While my father was out to do some shopping I phoned a friend in Brighton and found that not only did he have a room for rent, but there was a job available working with him in a new bookshop, if I wanted it. The moment for my departure was opportune.

My usual route home from the shop was a narrow, constricted one that afforded no views, or any impression of the size of the city that had been my home for a year and a half. For my last journey back to the apartment I turned right out of the shop door and made my way towards the Sacre Coeur. I took the streets that climbed upwards so that I would circle around the funicular railway and get the view that every holidaymaker in Paris made a point of appreciating. The pavements, then the roads themselves become choked with tourists, but they reminded me to value how pretty the area was; something I had almost forgotten. Familiarity had denied me the pleasure of the obvious picturesqueness of Paris, and it had taken my imminent departure from it to make me realise this.

On the steps of the Sacre Coeur, I looked over the heads of a large group of Japanese tourists at the view made misty by the pollution of the city. From where I stood, through the trees, I could see the Eiffel Tower, and I realised that in all my time in the city I had never even visited it. I was annoyed at all the hours I had spent in a "British" bookshop, on a dull side street, when I had left so much of Paris unexplored.

By the time I had got back to the bottom of the steps, however, and was passing the tourists sitting outside the restaurants on the rue Tardieu, my premature nostalgia had left me. The idea of packing and waiting alone in the apartment until my flight the next day depressed me. I was impatient for my journey home to begin.

The key that I was soon to give up let me into my apartment. Handley was standing just inside the door and before I could react he had grabbed my arm. He pulled me through to the living room where Hopper was sitting in the armchair, apparently studying the aquarium of fish.

On the coffee table in front of him lay a copy of *Hadrian the Seventh*. The spine was torn half off.

"What's wrong?" I asked.

Hopper was impassive: "It contained a radio transmitter."

For a moment I genuinely did not understand.

"Handley regularly sweeps the house for listening devices."

"Why?"

"My paranoia was justified. What I don't understand was why you brought it into my library."

"But I don't know anything about transmitters," I half-lied. I tried to argue, "Why would I want to bug your house?"

"I don't suppose that you would. But there are other people out there; other people who presumably persuaded you to plant it."

I gulped, and Hopper continued:

"I'm very disappointed. I mean, I understood your suspicions of me, and I was very forgiving of all the trouble you caused me with the police."

"But you've no proof that I had anything to do with the transmitter."

"Proof?" Hopper asked. "What's proof got to do with this? We're not in a court of law."

"I assure you, this is nothing to do with me."

"I'm not sure whether to believe you or not. I really don't know either way, but I don't like taking risks. Therefore I have to assume that you helped to plant this."

"What are you going to do?"

"You'll have to leave Paris."

"No problem! I've a flight booked for tomorrow. I'm going home to England."

"That's not good enough."

"Okay, I'll try to get a flight tonight. I can be packed and out of here in twenty minutes."

"I'm afraid that your departure will have to be left in the capable hands of Mr. Handley here."

"You can't believe what's written in that book!"

"Which book?" Hopper asked, standing up.

"*The Dark Return of Time.*"

"This has got nothing to do with any book."

He put out his hand, which I took without thinking.

"It's a shame," he said. "But you just couldn't leave things alone . . . There's no need to hurt him, Handley."

I had been scared before, but now I was petrified. Handley and I simply stood there, waiting for Hopper to leave. I started to shake. It took all my strength to say to Handley, "I'd like you to go now."

He was amused; it was the first time I'd seen him smile. All the skin over his bald head seemed to move.

I said firmly, "I'm going to call the police unless you leave right now."

I seemed to hear Handley saying, as if from a distance, "I've a friend in the police force who told me where to find the transmitter."

He advanced towards me, and I backed into the coffee table and fell over it. I put my arms out but when I fell I couldn't stop myself from hitting my head hard.

I woke up from being jolted around in the dark, not knowing where I was, or, for some moments, who I was. I decided to lie absolutely still until I had some idea of what was going on. I was aware that there had recently been movement, but now everything was quiet. There was a muffled sound of voices, but the direction from which they came was unclear.

My head hurt abominably. I realised that I was in a very confined space. There were two echoing thumps from close-by, then footsteps. I knew that under any other circumstances I would have been able to identify the sounds, but now I required some kind of reference to make sense of them.

There was a noise in front of me, and then a bright light. I closed my eyes and did my utmost not to move, although inwardly I cringed. Something metallic was removed from beside me and then there was a simultaneous change in pressure and a louder thump. The light had gone again and somebody was walking away over loose ground.

I realised that I was tied up in the back of a parked car.

I would have flailed around in panic, but it was too cramped. My heart raced. I could tell that my wrists and ankles were bound, and there was something over my mouth. I started to breathe too fast and couldn't get enough air. I was certain that I was about to die, but I was able to get my hands up together to my mouth and tear off the tape that covered it. It hurt, but fear anesthetised me. For a few seconds all I could do was gasp for air, but in that time I could see that, although the boot had been slammed down, there was now an irregular and indirect line of light in front of me.

I sensed that my captors were still close by, but carefully pushed at the lid of the boot. Although there was a little movement, it would not open, and so I felt along the edge, hoping I might find a catch. Before I realised what I'd done I'd released it and the lid had opened part way.

I decided that it was too much of a risk to wait and see if they'd noticed. I somehow pushed myself up and rolled over the edge and out. The fall knocked the wind out of me and, as I recognised the grey tape at my wrists and my ankles, panic overcame me again.

If I had been able to, I would certainly have made a run for it, even though we were in some flat, scrubby, sandy area with very little cover. I looked under the car and could see the legs of two men standing just a few yards away. It was a relief to hear that the tone of their conversation was relaxed.

I rolled over and got on to my haunches so that I could reach up and carefully pull the car boot back down.

Looking around, it was a desolate place, with far too much sky, and it would have been a miserable location in which to die. The thought encouraged me to action. There were several sharp stones embedded in the track, and I fell to my knees and used the most prominent of them to rub at the tape around my wrists. It took only three or four passes before it ripped and I was able to pull one hand free of the other. Trying not to think about the men, I rubbed the tape at my ankles against the same stone. This time it was more awkward, and took twice as long.

The moment I was free I again considered running, although I knew I wouldn't have been able to cover any distance before they noticed me. The sun was large and low in the sky, but it would still be light for some time and I would have no chance of hiding from them.

I checked back under the car and my heart leapt when I saw that the men were walking away. I moved cautiously around to the far side and watched them through the windows as they stopped fifty yards away. Handley was there with a spade, and Franklin was carrying a pickaxe. They spread out a little, staring down at the ground, testing it, and I could hear Franklin boasting to Handley that he wasn't afraid of manual labour. "But," he joked loudly, "if we can find a ready-made hole, it'll be better than having to dig a new one."

Looking through the car to where the men were standing, I knew that if I was going to run, I ought to let them do some digging and tire themselves out first. I had adrenalin and fear on my side, and so long as I made off at right angles to the track, they would have to follow on foot. As I worried about them using the car to pursue me I noticed that the keys were still in the ignition.

I had to act swiftly; again, there was no time to weigh up the advantages and disadvantages of action. I got in through the passenger door and, keeping my head down, moved across to the driver's seat. When I turned the ignition and depressed the accelerator and clutch, I didn't dare look over to the two thugs. With the car in first gear and the engine roaring I pulled away.

The wheels were spinning on the loose stones and sandy dirt, and when the engine was screaming I changed up to second. It was then that I heard two distinct thumps and the windscreen shattered. I punched a hole in the crazed glass and changed up to third as another thump came from the back of the car. In the rear-view mirror I could see that the back window was smashed and, through it, that the boot lid was moving up and down wildly. Beyond that was a maelstrom of dust.

I was going far too fast and nearly lost control of the car. It rocked on its suspension, and there were some horrible noises from underneath it. I tried to slow down, reasoning that Handley had no way of following me.

I had no idea where I was going; I only hoped that the track wouldn't come to a dead-end. It was perhaps a half mile before I came to a well-surfaced lane. Now I put on the seat belt, accelerated, and high hedges rushed by on either side. I only slowed down when I came up behind another car, so as to keep a discreet distance behind it and not be noticed. I realised what a mess my car was, and how it would attract attention.

An impressive château came into view, and then, at a junction with a busier road, I took the time to knock more of the broken glass out of the windscreen and squinted at the name of the town on the sign; Beauficel-en-Lyons. I had no idea where I was, and so just drove on.

The cold wind through the broken windscreen froze my hands and cheeks and made my eyes water. My attention was taken by the flapping boot lid, and so I took a small road off to the right, and after passing through another village I pulled in at a field gateway and stopped behind a hedge.

The position of the car was far too exposed for me to feel comfortable; there were fields all around, but I wasn't planning on staying for long. It also seemed too quiet; all I could hear was the ticking of the cooling car engine and the sound of a tractor in the distance. The sun was now molten on the horizon, staining everything a magnificent red gold. I went around to the back of the car and the first thing I noticed were two unmistakable bullet holes in it.

And I could see that something else was bundled up in the boot.

At first I thought that Candy was dead. Through her tangled black hair her face was a mess of blood and bruises and her t-shirt and trousers were blackened with blood and dirt. She was unconscious, but breathing. Shaking did not wake her.

I wasn't certain that I'd be able to get her out, and I considered closing the boot and driving straight to a hospital. As I wondered what to do, I heard the sound of running water coming from an overflowing drinking trough for animals next to the gate. I needed some kind of material, so I took off my pullover and dropped it into the icy cold water. When I wrung it out over Candy she woke up, tried to thrash around in panic, and then lay still, staring at me, full of fear.

"You're safe," I assured her. "They're not around. I'll help you."

I started to take the tape off her mouth and she squealed, so I ripped it off in one go and she was silent. After a moment she asked, "Where are we?"

"I've no idea."

It took a while to get Candy out of the boot. She was weak and so insubstantial. She protested and whined when I tore the tape at her wrists and ankles, in part because her skin was raw and bloody underneath from having been previously, tightly tied. As she sat on the ground I cleaned her up as best as I could and she submitted to my ministrations. She was wearing no make-up, her skin looked too white and mottled, and she had a horrible red mark over her mouth where I had pulled off the tape. Her eyes were worryingly dark-shadowed, but I felt an inappropriately-timed longing for her. Candy didn't speak, but when we heard a vehicle approach in the lane she stood up, as though about to run.

The car passed us without pausing. I noticed, however, that the tractor, now only one field over, had stopped, and we decided to leave. As I reversed the car out of the field I could see the farmer in the distance walking over to investigate.

The light of the sunset was draining away and night was gathering in the forest through which we drove. In a very small lay-by we stopped and I cleared the last of the glass from the windscreen. Candy had her eyes closed and was silent, but she was shaking with the cold. When I opened the glove compartment and pulled out a small book of maps she didn't move.

The signposts were hard to read without my glasses, but I worked out that we were driving towards somewhere called La Neuve-Grange. By the weak interior light of the car, I had difficulty searching for it on the maps. As I finally located the village I saw Candy put her hand into the glove compartment. She pulled out a heavy black handgun.

"Take me back to Paris," she said painfully.

"Please put that back."

She shook her head.

"Put it back while I'm driving, please," I said.

She nodded and asked, "Where are we, anyway?"

"North-west of Paris, I think. Perhaps one hundred kilometres away.'

"And what are we doing here?"

"Hopper's men were looking for a hole to bury us both in."

"How did we get away?"

"Pure fucking luck."

She grinned, but it pained her, which made her laugh again, and in relief I found myself doing the same. She reached over and held my hand tightly.

When we drove on, Candy tried to speak but I couldn't hear her properly for the noise of the wind through the open windscreen. Later on I realised she was crying.

I turned off the main road at somewhere called Frileuse because I was worried about being on such a major road. We passed an event at a large house; people were parking and getting out of their cars, but paid us no attention as we drove by.

"Stop," Candy said. "We'll steal a car."

"We can't. I don't know how, and they'd report it. At least Handley isn't going to complain to the police that his car's been stolen."

I pulled over and turned off the engine.

"Why have you stopped?"

"Because we need to decide what we're doing. If the police see us driving like this they're bound to pull us over. How do we explain that it isn't our car? I don't know what we'd say about the bullet holes, or why you've been beaten up, or why we've got a gun in the glove compartment."

"I need to get to Paris tonight, before Handley gets back. I'm going to take that gun and kill Hopper."

"That's madness."

"Is it? The bastard has had me tied up in his cellar for weeks. Handley's occasionally thrown me food and regularly beaten me. And you know very well he was going to kill me and dump me in a hole."

"Perhaps we should go to the police."

"Handley made it clear to me that they're in with the police."

"But it might just be bluff, or showing off. If we go into a police station and tell them what's happened what's the worst they can do to us?"

"They can hand us back over to Hopper and Handley."

"It's hardly likely, is it?"

"Isn't it?"

"I don't know."

"Just take me to Paris. Drop me off outside Hopper's and do what the hell you like. Go to the police if you want to, but give me time to kill Hopper."

"I want nothing to do with that."

"But you'll drive me there?"

"Handley will've called his boss."

"He won't expect me to come straight back to the house where he's had me locked up all this time. And you've got to go somewhere, so why not Paris?"

"I suppose that if we use the map, and take as many back roads as possible, we could do it. It's so bloody cold with no windscreen. My hands are freezing."

"You haven't had cold water poured all over you."

"Why don't we stop somewhere and try and get a hotel room, just for the night."

"And give Handley time to get back to Paris? Anyway, who'd let us into a hotel driving up in this car, looking like we do? Especially looking like I do! No, we have to go back to Hopper's tonight. It's the only chance I'll have."

It was an appalling journey. What should have been an hour-and-a-half's driving took more like four. Several times I had to stop and get the feeling back into my hands because they were so cold. Luck, however, was on our side and we didn't see any police cars at all, even in the very centre of Paris. At several junctions in the city I saw a few pedestrians stare at us, surprised at the lack of windscreen.

It was just past midnight when we finally found ourselves turning the car into rue St. Vincent.

"How are you going to get into the house?" I asked.

"With the gun," she said, and took it out of the glove compartment.

"What if he won't open the door to you?"

She didn't answer, and when I pulled up outside Hopper's house she didn't get out.

"Perhaps there's a back door," she said.

"There probably is, but at this time of night it'll be locked."

"Use the intercom. Say you're Handley."

"He won't fall for that. I don't sound like him. And Handley would probably have his own key. He might even have got back by now."

"Then I don't know what to do."

"We'll dump the car, and go and find a quiet hotel."

"No," she insisted, and continued to stare ahead, out of the glassless windscreen. In the streetlights I could see tears welling in her eyes and a great tenderness for her came over me. With numb fingers I brushed her hair from her frozen face.

The engine was still running and I would probably have driven away if I had known where to go. We sat there for another twenty seconds, saying nothing, before the front door to the house opened and Hopper himself appeared. He must have heard the car, and assumed that Handley had returned. When he saw us he looked confused for a moment and then Candy had raised the gun. She pointed it at him, past me, uncomfortably close to my face.

I looked back at Hopper, who had realised the danger he was in, but now Candy appeared calm, collected and in earnest. She kept the barrel level and told him to kneel down on the pavement, with his hands on his head, which he did. She manoeuvred herself backwards out of her door and was alongside him in a moment. I thought that she was going to execute him there and then, and he must have had the same fear.

"Inside the house," she insisted.

He got up awkwardly and she pushed him in front of her.

"Handley and his friends not back yet, I take it?" she taunted.

"No," he said, taking out his key and unlocking the door. "You appear to have their car."

I just wanted to drive away, but couldn't do so. I didn't feel I could call the police, either. Reluctantly I got out of the car and followed them through the wide open front door.

I followed the distant sound of Candy's voice. She appeared to have taken Hopper down some stairs into a cellar which, when I investigated, was comprised of two large rooms. The first contained cleaning equipment, some furniture, and several racks of wine. Candy and Hopper were in the further room which was almost entirely empty.

Candy half turned when she saw me. "Tie him to them," she ordered, pointing to a blank wall with climbers' hooks screwed into it. She was holding the gun to Hopper's head. "Then you can leave. Use those plastic ties—that's what they used on me."

There was a plastic bag of them spilling out over a bench.

"No," Hopper said. "I'm tired of this game."

He made a grab for the gun and it went off, an astonishingly loud and disorientating blast in the confined space.

Candy was suddenly lying on the floor next to me, still holding the weapon. Hopper had his hands to his head, shaking it, blinking.

"That was close," he said. Although my ears were ringing I could hear him say, "Now give it to me."

Candy was obviously bewildered, and so I took the gun from her.

"Stay there," I ordered Hopper. He moved towards me so I shouted the same thing again.

"Give me the gun, Flavian," he shouted back. "Otherwise I'll kill you both."

I held it in both hands, as I'd seen in films, and pointed at his head.

"You haven't got the guts," he said.

He was right. I couldn't kill him. And so I lowered the gun and fired at his knee.

The sound was deafening, and the recoil hurt. Hopper's leg was swept behind him and he pirouetted and fell awkwardly.

I stayed in the same position, the gun still trained on Hopper, and Candy stood up kissed me on the cheek. She walked over to where Hopper was alternately clutching at his leg and releasing it. She kicked him savagely in the side of the head.

"No!" I shouted, but she did it again and I had to pull her away.

"You've got to leave him to me," she shouted back.

"Come on, let's get out of here. Somebody will've heard us."

"The place is soundproofed; nobody ever heard me screaming."

"They wouldn't have left all the doors wide open like we have."

Candy took the gun from my hand. When she put it to Hopper's temple she demanded to know where the book was.

"In his safe," I answered for him.

"What else has he got in there?"

"I don't know. Money . . ."

"What's the combination?" she asked him, but he was in too much pain to listen. She hit him with the gun and screamed the question in his ear: "Safe combination, now."

"It has a key," I said, remembering that he had taken it from his waistcoat pocket before.

While she took it out I asked for the gun.

"I was never intending to shoot him," she said grimly, and handed it over with the ornate little key. "Go up and take everything from the safe. I'll follow you."

I was pleased to leave the cellar, and didn't want to think about what would be happening down there. I ran up to the library and to the fat old safe sitting squat and heavy on the floor by Hopper's desk. When I put down the gun my hands were shaking and it took me three attempts before I could open the door. I took out *The Dark Return of Time* and for only a moment considered leafing through it. Instead, I concentrated on pulling out bags of cash onto the floor. I told myself not to question what the hell I was doing; I didn't have the leisure to debate the matter. Instead, I wondered how we would carry away all the money. There was a noise behind me and I turned to see one of Hopper's other men standing in the doorway, looking confused.

Whatever he was saying, with my damaged hearing I couldn't make it out. I picked up the gun and pointed it at him, and he put up his hands.

"I need some bags," I yelled, and he nodded in the direction of a cupboard near the door.

"Get them out for me, slowly." I guessed that I was shouting, but hoped that it made me sound more threatening. The man was very wary, but did as I told him. He brought out two large black hold-alls, and I watched over him as he filled them with the contents of the safe.

"And the book," I said, and watched him place it on the top of one of the open bags.

"I'll just lie on the ground," he said. 'And you can go. I won't move."

I took the hold-alls, one at a time, to the door, covering the man with the gun all the while. As I finished there came a horrible scream from downstairs. A minute passed before Candy appeared from the cellar.

"Have you got everything," she asked. She had fresh blood on her shirt and she looked determined.

"Everything, yes."

"Okay," she said grimly, picking up one of the bags. "Let's go."

I hadn't considered that there would be anyone out in the street, but five or six concerned-looking people were standing around the car. With its bullet holes, missing windscreen, open doors and idling engine it had attracted attention. They all moved away quickly as we exited the house, noticing the gun that I was carrying.

I wrenched open the back door and threw my bag inside. Candy threw hers in after it, and then the shooting started.

I instinctively pushed Candy inside after the bags, and I jumped in at the driver's seat.

There was the repeated loud retort of a gun and the seemingly disassociated *crump, crump, crump* of bullets penetrating the car. Without even trying to close the door, I put it into first gear and it leapt forward. I didn't know who was firing, or where from, but as I reached the Lepin Agile crossroads I heard another retort and felt something hit the side of my head. For a second I lost control of the car and it screeched around on the brick setts in the road and bounced off a parked car. Somehow we had turned through almost 360 degrees and were still pointing in the right direction, but the engine had stalled. As I restarted the car there came the sound of more bullets entering the bodywork. The door slammed shut on its own as I drove past another car fast and wild down the narrow street.

I tore around Avenue Junot and negotiated the kink up rue Norvins without slowing. I had to think how to get out of Montmartre and head in a direction that I hoped was south, taking care not to drive too fast now that the immediate danger was over. When I was crossing the Avenue de Fontainbleu I saw a brightly-lit Shell petrol station and remembered what Candy had said earlier that evening about stealing a car. I pulled in alongside a pump as a woman had just finished filling up a small Fiat.

I picked the gun out of the foot-well of the passenger seat, got out of our wreck, and as she saw me the woman screamed.

"*Votre voiture,*" I shouted, and she handed me the keys.

It was only then that I saw that Candy was still slumped in the back seat of Hopper's car.

"Are you okay?" I asked.

She grimaced, "Where are we?"

"We needed a new vehicle. Come on."

She had to be helped out of the car and into the passenger seat of the Fiat. When I went to get the bags from the old car I noticed the blood where she had been lying.

As we drove off, pulling back on to the avenue, I could hear distant sirens and so I turned left, then right and left again until we were finally on the Boulevard de Stalingrad. I tried to drive at a reasonable speed again, now heading north.

Candy said, though her teeth: "We should've at least tied up that man in the library. We should've shot him."

"I couldn't. I can't kill people like you can."

"I've never succeeded in killing anyone before. Was that Handley and the other men shooting at us outside the house?" she asked.

"I suppose so. I didn't have time to look."

"Shooting Hopper would've been too quick. I slit both his wrists, up the veins, so he could watch himself bleed to death. There's a lot of blood down in that cellar. But his men will get him medical help."

"You've a pretty poor record as a murderer."

"I have," she replied grimly. "*We'll* probably die first."

"Were you shot? There was a lot of blood in the backseat of Hopper's car."

"Yes. There's now quite a lot in this one."

The light was poor, but she appeared to be clutching Hopper's book, and in the streetlights it seemed to be even more stained than before.

"I'll take you to a hospital."

"And get handed over to the police? No."

"If you pass out I'm getting you some help."

"I'll be all right," she said, but I could see her grimacing again.

"So where are we going?"

At that moment I decided that we should go back to my apartment on the rue André Antoine, reasoning that it would be too obvious a place for anyone to look for us. I knew that good counter-arguments could be made, but I didn't want to have to think any more.

Negotiating the streets as they became more familiar gave an illusion and semblance of normality, but when I parked on the corner, where the rue André Antoine turns into rue Véron, everything felt wrong. I waited until I was sure there was nobody around and then tried to get Candy out of the car. The disembodied shouts of late-night revellers, and the distant sounds of vehicles, echoed down the streets towards us, but nobody came.

Candy was losing her strength. I had to pick her out of the passenger seat and half-carry her to the door. That was too much for her, though, and she had to be carried up the four floors to the apartment. It was like holding a tired child who had been playing in a dressing-up box full of clothes far too big for her; she seemed to have become so insubstantial. Once inside, I laid her on the bed and she waved back up at me weakly, distantly. I said I'd return as soon as I could. I locked her into the apartment and went down to the car.

Driving gave me something else to think about. At the Boulevard de Clichy I turned left and then just drove. I had it in mind to leave the car on one of the roads around the park at the end of rue Manin, hoping that it might be a while before it was discovered. However, when I was only a few streets away the priorities changed and the road veered in another direction. I was overcome with frustration and tiredness, and just wanted the nightmare to stop. A car pulled out in front of me from between two buildings and I drove into the space it had vacated. I thought about setting light to the Fiat, but it was too dangerous. I didn't have any matches anyway, and, above all else, I no longer cared.

A Metro station wasn't very far, but I decided to start walking back the way that I had come. I wanted to formulate a plan by the time I returned to the apartment. On the way I considered calling for an ambulance for Candy and giving them my address, but as I came to a public telephone I couldn't bring myself to do it. I simply walked on, and continued walking.

III.

In the headlights of a passing car I looked down and saw for the first time that my clothes were drenched in Candy's blood. Paranoia overcame me, and as I made my way back to the apartment I sought out the shadows that eluded the strategically-placed street lamps and the lights from shop windows. Even the night sky glowed above me, but there were still some areas of darkness that allowed me to pass, I hoped, unnoticed. For a while I followed a scrawny fox and, just as it did, I kept myself close to the walls as I walked, and hurried through any area that was too well-lit and open. Not that anyone cared; the occasional people I passed were mainly young and often drunk, in groups or alone, on their way to or from clubs. Their laughter was raucous, but only seemed too loud because there was so much space for the noise to fill. The emptiness of the streets meant that the infrequent cars seemed to be driving past at an excessive speed, but that suited me.

It was disconcerting not to be fighting through people on the city streets, or at least making allowances for others. My path was unhindered, but though I could move forward with ease I deliberately walked at an even, measured pace. I didn't want to be faced with more decisions.

I slowed my steps further, dawdling, but almost against my will I was back at the rue André Antoine. Unforgiving fluorescent lights came on in the hallway when I entered my building, and on the stairs they showed up the spots of blood that led a trail right up to my own front door. The sight of the blood, repeated step after step, cleared my mind. I knew what I had to do; what I should have done an hour before. I let myself into the apartment and went straight through to the bedroom, resolved to call for an ambulance.

I flicked on the bedroom light, but Candy was not on the bed. It was simply a mess of sheets smeared with blood. Sitting on a chair by the window was Handley, his gun pointing at me.

"Where is she," I demanded.

He shrugged and said, "Dealt with. Like I'm about to deal with you. But first, tell me where the book is, and where I can find the money from the safe. Then I'll make your death quick and painless."

As he spoke I wondered what chance I would have if I ran for the door. I had nothing to lose, but I also realised that so long as he wanted something from me; he wasn't going to shoot me.

"I'll tell you if you let me and Candy go free."

"It's too late for Candy," he said, and put the gun to his own head for a moment. Quietly he said, "Bang."

I should have taken my chance to run while the gun wasn't aimed in my direction.

"You'll be interested to learn that Reginald Hopper is still alive," he said. "We got back just in time. He's not happy; he's in a lot of pain. He wants the book and the money returned. I'm not happy either; you made a fool out of me."

"The money's in a car we stole, a Fiat. I parked it somewhere off the Boulevard de Clichy. I couldn't tell you the street name. Thinking about it, I'm not sure I even remembered to lock it."

He got up carefully, the direction of his gun never wavering.

"I understand why you want the money, but what's so special about the book?" I asked.

"I'm not going to waste my time on explanations. Not when I'm going to kill you? Where is it?"

"Safe, where you won't find it," I bluffed. "I realise that the book explains Hopper's past. Is it his biography, or autobiography? I want to talk to him, not his staff."

The man laughed.

"As you are going to die I might as well tell you. I've seen inside the book and it's about me."

"I don't understand."

"No, you wouldn't. You see, he was my boss, but I'm the one who came to Paris and needed to launder a lot of money from the sale of a bullion robbery. His businesses here were doing badly and I came to give him a hand; I helped to turn things around. *I* don't work for *him*!"

"Well, that's how it looks to everyone else."

"Well, it's convenient that way. Now, where's the book?"

"If you let me go . . . " I started to say and then he hit me with the gun. I saw a flash and the pain made my head ring.

Handley pushed me down and stood over me, his foot raised above my chest.

"Tell me where the book's hidden, and you'll feel no pain," he said. "Refuse to tell me, and I'll break your ribs."

"Candy had it."

"Not when I got here, she didn't." He considered this; "So is it still here, in this apartment?"

"I don't know."

"Up!" he commanded, and I did as I was told. "Start looking!"

I was sure that Handley was going to hit me again so I went to the chest of drawers and pulled open the first drawer, which he told me to empty on the ground. When they were all empty he wanted the chest itself moved away from the wall and turned over. He made me do the same with the bedside tables and then the free-standing cupboard. As I carried out his commands there came a banging on the floor from the neighbours below, but Handley ignored them and told me to continue.

"Who wrote the book?" I asked as he pushed me into the living room. At least I was still alive.

"How would I know? Candy's father told Hopper about it and Hopper told me, but I couldn't find it after Smith died and Hopper was shot. I'd decided it was a wind-up, but then it turned up in Saint-Quentin."

"Did Candy put it in the sale?"

"It was no coincidence that your father found out about it, or that Candy was at the sale."

"I still don't understand."

"Stop talking and keep looking!"

I could not find the book. Handley was trying to keep calm, insisting that I turn everything upside down and inside out, and also that I keep the noise to a minimum. It was obvious that he didn't know what to do. His anger increased and in frustration he kicked at the aquarium. The glass cracked and collapsed, and water and fish cascaded out over the floor. Moments later there were people outside the door, hammering on it.

If it wasn't the police, then I reasoned that at least the arrival of neighbours might diffuse the situation. Handley ordered me back into the bedroom and I told him he'd better leave. Instead, he pushed me down on the bed. I raised my head and was surprised to see among the sheets the very book he was after!

I didn't have time to say anything. Handley picked up a pillow and used it to push my head down on top of the book. For a moment I saw Candy standing on the other side of the room, or was it Corrina? I called out to her but

Handley fired the single shot that went through the pillow, my head, and *The Dark Return of Time*.

Epilogue

The odds of surviving a bullet through the head are very long, but people are known to recover. The effects can vary tremendously. As a result of the damage to his brain, Reginald Hopper was supposed to have suffered complete memory loss. My circumstances were somewhat different.

I spent a month on a high dependency unit in hospital and underwent a number of operations. Somehow I survived, with impairment to my eyesight being the biggest long-term problem. Many of my motor functions, including speech, were affected, but I recovered most of them, over time, with the help of physiotherapy.

As soon as I was able to communicate I became frustrated because the one faculty I had managed to maintain, with great clarity, was my memory. It seemed to take forever before I could explain to people what had happened to me. And then I was moved from Paris to London.

For several months I was under the care not only of doctors and physiotherapists, but also a psychiatrist. When I asked why, I was told that such an experience as I had survived would leave anyone with emotional problems. The psychiatrist listened to me talk about the events in Paris for hours at a time, yet it was infuriating that I was only able to explain the same matters to the police on one occasion. Over time it was firmly and carefully explained to me that none of the events that I remembered could have happened. I was told that I had simply disturbed an armed burglar in my apartment.

There was no choice but to agree with the story, although the details, as I remembered them, remained sharply-etched in my mind. I decided that there might be reasons why the various authorities would go to some length to keep the whole case quiet. I decided that I would go along with their explanation, although I resented their approach: all that I required was for somebody to say that I was not mistaken, albeit that it couldn't be officially admitted.

After my release from hospital I moved back with my mother to our old family house in Edgeware. She nursed me unfailingly, and from the outset I knew how wrong I had been to blame her for Corrina's death. She had lost weight and a great deal of her spirit since the accident. I burst into tears when I saw the photo of me and Corrina framed by her bedside. Holding her responsible was too easy; if I had not found an excuse, my mother would not have been driving Corrina to work the morning she hit black ice and crashed.

My father visited several times. On his first evening we were alone in the front room and I made reference to Hopper, Candy, and *The Dark Return of Time*. When he appeared to be confused by my remarks I pressed him, giving specific details; dates and addresses. But still he insisted that nothing of what I claimed had ever happened. He was my one potential ally, but he refused to help me.

When I had recovered ninety percent of my health I told my mother that I wished to visit Paris. She didn't know why, but my father did. He sent me photographs of rue André Gill and the south side of the rue St. Vincent. Although the streets looked familiar, neither Candy's building nor Hopper's house seemed to be standing. Of course, where Candy lived had been destroyed by fire and would have been rebuilt, but where Hopper's house should have been there appeared to be tall trees and a wild garden.

Nevertheless, I insisted on travelling to Paris, and my mother was adamant that she would accompany me. Together, on a brilliantly blue summer day, we flew from Heathrow to Charles de Gaulle airport. It was strange being back in the city; the familiarity of it all seemed to validate specific memories that others wanted to deny.

When we were unpacked, my mother and I walked over to Bennett's British Bookshop and I found it almost completely unchanged. As I wandered around the shelves I recognised more than half of the stock, and the books on the poetry shelf did not appear to have altered at all since I had re-arranged them nearly three years before. I was seeking evidence, but it was not to be found: in the crime section, although there were several books by Ruth Rendell, there was no first American edition of *A Demon in My View*.

We ate at the café in Le Bateau-Lavoir. It was a mixture of Parisians and tourists and was busy but friendly. We did not talk about what had happened to me, but reminisced about the days when we had all lived together in the house in Edgeware. It was another existence that we discussed, made all the more remote by geographical distance.

"You had a happy childhood, didn't you?" asked my mother, and I was upset to see in her eyes just how much she craved that reassurance. I told her that I had.

My father paid the patron with the startling beard, and we parted in the tree-filled, prettily-illuminated square. It was a beautiful night, and I told my mother that we could go back to the hotel by walking down the rue des Saules. She was chattering away, as she often does after a few glasses of wine, and was content to let me take her along rue St. Vincent.

I stopped outside Hopper's house and took out of my pocket the photograph my father had sent me. My eyesight wasn't good, but I had studied the photo before and knew that somebody had done a very professional job of taking the house out of the image and replacing it with trees. With modern technology any image can be faked, but there, in rue St. Vincent, the evidence was before me. My mother was becoming tiresome, though. She wasn't interested. She wanted to know whether it was a private or public garden in front of us, and pointing upwards she asked if the birds were crows, rooks, or ravens. It was as though she couldn't see what was before her very eyes.

About the Author

R. B. Russell co-runs independent UK publisher Tartarus Press with Rosalie Parker. Ray's fiction has been published in four short story collections, three novellas and three novels. He has also published a biography of Robert Aickman, and a bibliographical memoir, *Fifty Forgotten Books*. Based in the Yorkshire Dales since 2000, Ray and Rosalie have a grown-up son, Tim.

SWAN RIVER PRESS

Founded in 2003, Swan River Press is an independent publishing company, based in Dublin, Ireland, dedicated to gothic, supernatural, and fantastic literature. We specialise in limited edition hardbacks, publishing fiction from around the world with an emphasis on Ireland's contributions to the genre.

www.swanriverpress.ie

"While small publishers often produce beautiful books, few can match those from Swan River Press."

– Washington Post

"It [is] often down to small, independent, specialist presses to keep the candle of horror fiction flickering . . ."

– The Irish Times

"Swan River Press—cutting edge of New Gothic."

– Joyce Carol Oates

"The redoubtable Brian J. Showers [keeps] the myriad voices of Irish fantasy alive there in Dublin."

– Alan Moore

GHOSTS

R. B. Russell

Ghosts contains R. B. Russell's debut publications, *Putting the Pieces in Place* and *Bloody Baudelaire*. Enigmatic and enticing, they combine a respect for the great tradition of supernatural fiction, with a chilling contemporary European resonance. With original and compelling narratives, Russell's stories offer the reader insights into the more hidden, often puzzling, impulses of human nature, with all its uncertainty and intrigue. There are few conventional shocks or horrors on display, but you are likely to come away with the feeling that there has been a subtle and unsettling shift in your understanding of the way things are. This book is a disquieting journey through twilight regions of love, loss, memory and ghosts. This volume contains "In Hiding", which was shortlisted for the 2010 World Fantasy Awards.

*"Russell's stories are captivating for their
depth of mystery and haunting melancholy."*

– Thomas Ligotti

"Russell deals in possibilities beyond the rational."

– Rue Morgue

*"Quiet horror told in an unassuming,
polished narrative style."*

– Hellnotes

DEATH MAKES
STRANGERS OF US ALL

R. B. Russell

At the edges of everyday life, on geographical boundaries and in the margins of society, certainties and realities can wear thin. And if we find ourselves in such occult and outland territory late at night, we might glimpse phenomena out of the corner of our eye that cannot possibly be there. At such times even the past, apparently fixed and unchanging in memories and dreams, cannot be relied upon.

But what happens if we find ourselves passing beyond even these frayed perimeters of life? Can others follow us, or are we on our own? And just where will our final journey take us? How can we perceive or understand the changes that death will bring?

*"The disorienting title story of R. B. Russell's superb
Death Makes Strangers of Us All takes us into
an 'unreal city' straight out of Kafka or Borges."*

– Michael Dirda, *Washington Post*

*"Once again, R. B. Russell has produced
a fine collection of remarkable stories
told in a captivating, styling fashion."*

– Mario Guslandi

SPARKS FROM THE FIRE

Rosalie Parker

The stories in *Sparks from the Fire* explore a wide variety of familiar characters and settings, yet there is always something else—a shadow world that haunts, disturbs, and threatens. Sons and daughters, mothers and fathers, recluses and lovers—all find themselves shifting between realities: the prosaic and the mystical, even between life and death. The horrors and wonders of these parallel existences are often glimpsed, sometimes revealed, and occasionally overwhelm. These nineteen tales inhabit a terrain in which the uncanny may at any time intrude into everyday life.

"[Parker's] treatment of the fantastic is often so light and ambiguous that stories in which it does manifest are of a piece with tales such as 'Jetsam' and 'Job Start', sensitive character sketches whose celebration of life's unforeseen surprises will appeal to fantasy fans as much as the book's more overtly uncanny tales. Parker proves herself a subtle and versatile writer."

– Publishers Weekly

"If you prefer spending dark evenings with a single author, consider . . . Rosalie Parker's Sparks From the Fire, *which collects nineteen stories, some set against the brooding Yorkshire landscape."*

– Michael Dirda, *Washington Post*